# Brown-Eyed Girl

# Denise Devine

*USA Today Bestselling Author*

A Sweet Small Town Romance

West Loon Bay Series

Book Two

Wild Prairie Rose Books

# Brown-Eyed Girl

(West Loon Bay Series – Book 2)

Print Edition

Copyright 2022 by Denise Devine

https://www.deniseannettedevine.com

ISBN: 978-1-943124-37-4

Published in the United States of America

Wild Prairie Rose Books

Cover Design by Raine English

# Want to stay in touch with me?

Sign up for my newsletter at https://eepurl.com/csOJZL and receive a *free novella*. You'll be the first to know about my new releases, sales and special events.

Denise Devine

Tremolo – the laughing call of a loon

# Prologue

The wedding reception of Annika Nilsen and Alexander Lange

Morganville, Enchanted Island of the United States

East Caribbean Sea

The warm August evening enveloped Carly Strand with a delicate breeze as she sat at the head table at her best friend's wedding reception, listlessly picking at a slice of cake.

Annika's small but intimate wedding had unfolded like a scene in a fairytale. Walking down the aisle on her father's arm, she glowed with happiness and the promise of a wonderful life to come. A diamond tiara gleamed on the crown of her shimmering blonde hair. Her ivory silk dress, long and gently flared, swayed gracefully as she walked. Her bouquet, a large cascade of white and mango calla lilies accented with white jasmine and ribbons had been almost too large for her to hold.

As Annika's maid of honor, Carly should have been enchanted and inspired by such a magical evening. Why then did she feel so drained? So empty?

Anxious to avoid attention, she glanced around looking for an inconspicuous exit to disappear through once the dance started. People would be having so much fun, it would be easy for her to slip away unnoticed and retreat to her room.

She glanced around, looking for a spot in the shadows to sit, making her getaway that much easier. Overhead, purple bougainvillea vines grew along the balconies lining the interior walls of the open-air courtyard of the historic Morganville Hotel. In one corner, flanked by potted palms and ruby hibiscus, a carved stone fountain quietly bubbled. Soft lighting ribboned with flowing white tulle under the balconies cast a romantic glow across the small group of family and close friends. The sweet, exotic scent of jasmine and the music of steel drums filled the balmy evening air with enchantment.

She sighed. Just short of crawling under the table, there was nowhere to go until the music started.

Seating for the wedding party at dinner followed the male/female tradition. Alex, the groom sat at the center of the head table. Annika sat at his left and the best man sat next to her. As the maid of honor, Carly sat on the groom's right which suited her just fine. The farther she sat from his best man, the better!

From the corner of her eye, she watched curiously as Alex whispered a few words to Annika and then promptly left the table. Annika slid onto his empty chair and leaned toward Carly, curving her arm around Carly's shoulders.

"Hey, sweetie," Annika said with care in her voice, "is something wrong? You don't seem like yourself tonight."

"I'm just tired, that's all. It's been a long day," Carly responded. She put on a cheerful expression, but behind her forced smile, tears threatened to fall. She loved Annika dearly and was delighted that her best friend had finally found her "happily ever after" with the man of her dreams. Sadly, nothing could fill the deep well of Carly's loneliness. Nothing short of a miracle, anyway.

"Where did Alex go?" Carly asked, deliberately changing the subject.

Annika stared across the room to where her new husband stood in a black tuxedo talking to the lead singer of the Jamaican band. "He wants to change the song for our first dance, but he wouldn't tell me what he's chosen. It's a surprise." She laughed. "Get your dancing shoes on, girl. The entertainment is about to begin."

Carly suspected what Annika had on her mind. "About the wedding party..." She swallowed hard. "Paired together as couples, I mean—"

"It's just one dance, Carly." Annika grabbed a knife and cut a small piece off of the corner of Carly's cake. Picking it up with her fingers, she popped it into her mouth. "You and Erik can put your feud aside for that long, can't you? For me?"

"It's not a feud," Carly argued. "We just don't...have anything to say to each other."

She glanced past Annika to Erik Nilsen, Annika's older brother, who also happened to be Alex's best man. Sitting at the opposite end of the table, Erik looked tired and bored as he checked his watch for the umpteenth time. A gentle breeze blew his thick hair across his forehead. The frown on his face suggested he would rather be lying on one of Enchanted Island's beautiful beaches in shorts and a T-shirt instead of sitting here in a hot tuxedo. If so, she heartily agreed with him, but she had no intention of telling him so. What was there to say to the guy who long ago had shattered her heart into a million pieces?

"That's not really what I intended to talk to you about," Annika said sincerely. "I've said this before, but I want you to know how very sorry I am about canceling our girls' trip out west at the last minute. I mean it, Carly. I know it deeply hurt your feelings when I backed out. I promised you with all my heart that I'd go and then I let you down."

"It's okay, Annika," Carly replied, eager to show that she held no grudge. "If a guy like Alex had fallen in love with me and asked me not to go, I'd have done the same thing."

The puzzled look in Annika's wide, blue eyes indicated she found that statement puzzling. She leaned close. "What about Erik," she whispered as she angled her head in her brother's direction. "He keeps asking me about you, but I don't know what to tell him. He doesn't understand why you're avoiding him. You guys used to be sweethearts."

Carly shook her head as her ire rose. "That will *never* happen again."

Alex suddenly appeared at the table, wanting his chair back. Tall, dark-haired, and ruggedly handsome, Alexander Lange's past relationships included high-fashion models and Hollywood starlets, but from the moment they met, he'd only had eyes for his best friend's little sister.

"Only because you don't *want* it to," Annika muttered. Licking a glob of frosting off her finger, she smiled at Alex and slid back to her own chair.

A drum roll garnered everyone's attention. "Ladies and gentlemen, this is the moment you've all been waiting for. Let's welcome Mr. and Mrs. Alexander Lange to the dance floor!"

Alex took Annika by the hand to a raucous round of applause and led her to the center of the stone floor. He took her in his arms and gazed lovingly into her eyes as he pulled her close and began to dance to the music of Unchained Melody.

Carly sat with her hands gripping the edge of her chair, dreading the moment she and Erik would have to dance in front of the entire group. The thought of his long, muscular arms around her, holding her close made a cold sweat break out on the back of her neck.

Ever since Erik and Alex moved back to their small town of West Loon Bay, Minnesota, Carly had managed to avoid Erik. Now she was forced to reunite with him in the worst possible way. Dancing cheek to cheek.

*I can't do this*, she thought desperately as a lump formed in her throat. *I feel sick.*

A sip of water helped calm her down through the bride and groom's dance but when the lead singer announced that the wedding party would join the newlyweds and their parents, Carly's heart began to slam in her chest.

Strong, gentle fingers encircled her arm, urging her to rise from the chair. She looked up and found Erik's tall, brawny form towering over her. Physically, he hadn't changed much since they dated in high school. An offensive lineman on their school football team, he'd been quite the catch back in the day with thick reddish-brown hair and deep blue eyes. He leaned forward, his eyes reflecting a mixture of curiosity and uncertainty. "It's okay, Carly," he whispered. "I don't bite. I just want to dance with you."

With his help, she stood, but her knees shook so badly they threatened to buckle underneath her. He led her to the dance floor and tentatively slid his arms around her, supporting her. Slowly, they moved in unison to the music.

*I can't breathe...* she thought as she allowed him to guide her around the stone floor. *He has no idea how much damage he has done to me. To my life.*

"You look beautiful tonight," he commented with a sincere smile as if trying to distract her from her unease. His remark had been uttered as a compliment but even so, it made her feel self-conscious in her strapless mango-colored gown.

"I'm sure you say that to all your women," she replied and sucked in a deep breath, acutely aware of his large palm resting on the small of her back. The touch of his fingers on her skin tingled, creating an earthquake of tiny shock waves shooting up her spine.

He pulled back, surprised. "What do you mean by that?"

"Don't play your games with me," she countered bluntly. "For the past decade, you and Alex have toured with your rock band all over the world. You've been photographed and linked with more beautiful women than Alex has—and that's saying something."

He mulled over that for a few moments. "That's over now. I left the celebrity life behind for a reason. Alex and I both did once we came to our senses and realized that the most important things in life aren't money and fame. It's family. The one you were born into and the one you eventually create."

Her nervous laugh cut through the air. "So, are you saying that you're going to find your soulmate in West Loon Bay, population three hundred and ninety-seven?"

"That's right," he replied gazing intently into her eyes. "If she'll have me."

She glared back at him, angry and hurt at his nerve. She wasn't good enough for him ten years ago when he abandoned her, one month before her eighteenth birthday. In all that time, he could have contacted her, but he was too busy enjoying the women lining up at his concerts to "get lucky" with him to spare the time. Did he really think she was stupid enough to think they could simply pick up where they'd left off? "Good luck with that," she snapped.

He stopped dancing and gripped her by the arms. "I don't understand you, Carly. You've been avoiding me ever since I came back. I ask you to dance and you act as though my mere presence offends you. Why do you hate me so much?"

"I don't hate you, Erik," she said slowly. "I just never want to be hurt by you ever again."

She pulled away and walked off the dance floor before he could see her tears fall.

# Chapter One

West Loon Bay, Minnesota

Late September

The golden afternoon sun beat down upon the crystal blue water of Lake Tremolo as Erik lay on a full-length lounger under the Bimini top covering his pontoon with a notebook in one hand and a chilled bottle of beer in the other. He'd cut the engine a thousand feet from shore and dropped the anchor, hoping the gentle, methodical rocking of the watercraft on the waves would either inspire him to finish a new song or lull him to sleep. To his dismay, it did neither.

Wearing a T-shirt and shorts, he stretched out on the comfortable beige lounger and took a swig of his beer as he stared across the water. Dense woods covered the craggy shoreline of the huge lake, brilliantly displaying a patchwork of gold, scarlet and dark reds. His sister Annika, whom he collaborated with, had given him a sheet of paper this morning containing a set of lyrics for a new song. She called her work "poems," but to Erik, they were simply a collection of words that he turned into a ballad in the band's unique style. The finished product was handed off to Alex to compose the melody.

He'd been staring at the words on the page for an hour, waiting for inspiration, but nothing had come to mind. Instead, thoughts of Carly as a seventeen-year-old haunted him like a ghost from the past.

He took out the senior class photo of her that he kept in his wallet. The one he'd carried with him for the last ten years. Wrinkled and dog-eared, it still captured the sparkle in her large brown eyes. Her long, thick hair, the color of rich cocoa, glistened to her elbows and accentuated her curvy shape. Her wide, genuine smile never ceased to light up the lonely, dark corners of his heart.

Whenever his morale hit a low point on the road, he'd stare at her picture. The possibility that someday they could rebuild their friendship again would always lift his spirits. The way they'd broken up had torn his heart in two but made it easier to leave town and never look back. Through the years, he'd assumed she'd found happiness with someone else, but was surprised to find out that she had never married.

*She's so bitter,* he thought regretfully. *As though she's been badly hurt. I'd give anything to turn her pain into joy, but she won't even talk to me.*

He thought about the chilly spring night Carly's dad caught them together in the back of his van. She was seventeen—he was nineteen. Dan Strand was so angry he banned Erik from seeing her ever again. Erik never got the chance to tell her he was leaving town to take his band on a quest for a better future.

*I should have tried to keep in contact with her after we went on the road,* he thought, feeding his guilty conscience. *Time had always been on our side. Once the band became a success, I could have brought her on tour with me. We would have seen the world together.*

Shoulda, coulda, woulda! It didn't do any good to brood over it now.

The notebook slipped from his lap and landed on the floor as he closed his eyes, mulling over how much his life had changed since he, Alex, and three of their lifelong friends decided to hit the road with their band and never look back. Except lately, that's all he'd been doing…

He had gone on the road with Alex, Jonas, Gunnar, and Gabe to play their music and make a name for themselves. Never in their wildest imagination had they anticipated their hard rock band "Wolfmoon" would experience the ultra-stardom they'd achieved with double-platinum success on album after album.

For the first couple of years after they became famous, their lives played out like a dream come true. Their success and the money that came with it filled their bank accounts and plastered their faces on the covers of magazines all over the world. Eventually, though, the parties, women, and drugs began to lose their luster. The constant pressure of producing new material and touring to promote it wore them down. Alex developed migraines, Jonas had stomach problems, Gabe and Gunnar became depressed and he lost his ability to create fresh material. They knew they needed a break but the people surrounding them—the ones making the most money off them—kept pushing them to keep going until one night Alex collapsed—and along with him, their self-destructive lifestyle.

Last May, they'd returned to their roots, a tiny Minnesota tourist town poised on the shores of a huge, beautiful lake to reconnect with their families and take a much-needed hiatus before deciding their next steps as a band. No one expected Alex to fall in love with Annika. That sudden turn of events had changed everything again—including delaying the decision of when to go back on the road.

*That's fine with me,* Erik thought with a sigh. The idea of going on another tour and operating at the frenetic pace they once found exhilarating simply exhausted him now.

The shrill ring of his phone startled him. He reached down to grab it off the floor, causing him to nearly knock his beer out of its cupholder. The name "Jonas Strom" spread across the screen.

Erik sat up, resting his elbows on his knees. "Hey, what's going on?"

"I'm at your house standing on the dock. Your mom said you'd taken the pontoon out by yourself," Jonas replied sounding puzzled that he'd go alone. "You gonna be back soon?"

Erik grabbed his beer and drained the bottle. "Maybe. Why?"

"I'm bored," Jonas said. "I came by to see your new pontoon. Talk about a few things."

The edgy way in which Jonas' deep voice said *"talk about a few things"* caught Erik's attention. Jonas had something on his mind.

"Okay," Erik said as he dropped his empty bottle into a recycling container. "I'm on my way."

After he pulled up the anchor, he slid into the seat at the helm and started up the engine, heading back to shore.

Jonas stood at the end of the dock wearing jeans and a gray T-shirt with Prince's purple unisex symbol on it, talking on his phone as Erik slowly pulled up and turned off the engine. Jonas slipped his phone into his jean pocket and grinned. "So, this is your new toy, huh? I figured you were a fancy speedboat kind of guy."

"I am," Erik replied with a chuckle. "I bought this for my dad." He made a sweeping motion with his arm to showcase Knut's new luxury watercraft. "Dad can fish and listen to the baseball game in style. It makes for a nice little party barge, too."

Nodding his approval, Jonas stepped into the pontoon and sat down on one of the rear-facing loungers. "Nice. Take me for a ride."

Erik drove the pontoon slowly around the lake for twenty minutes and then stopped in the vicinity of where he'd been before Jonas called. "You want a beer?"

"Nah, too early," Jonas replied as Erik dropped the anchor. "Just give me a Coke. You got a cold one?"

"Sure thing." Erik grabbed two chilled cans from his cooler. "So," he said as he handed one to Jonas and pulled the tab on his can. "What did you want to talk about?"

"Like I told you on the phone, I'm bored," Jonas stated in a disillusioned tone. "There's nothing to do in this one-horse town and I'm getting antsy to get back on the road."

"You were the one who pushed the hardest for everyone to come back. Now you want to leave already?" Erik relaxed on the other lounger, stretching out his legs. The pontoon gently rocked on the water. "Where is this coming from?"

"Everything has changed so much," Jonas argued and took a swig of his Coke as he stared across the lake. "It's not the same place I left. Most of the guys I knew from school have moved away and all the girls who stuck around are married with a bazillion kids. I don't feel like I fit in here anymore."

Erik laughed softly. "Dude, we've been gone for ten years. What did you expect?"

"I don't know," Jonas answered and ran his hand through a riot of thick, dark curls, "but I didn't expect to find myself a stranger in my own hometown. I think it's time to move on."

"What?" Erik stared at him, totally flummoxed. "Where are you going?"

"Back to Anaheim, maybe. Or Chicago." Jonas shrugged; his expression turned downcast as he stared across the lake. "I haven't decided yet."

"You're considering leaving the band?" Erik bolted upright and swung his legs over the side of the lounger. "Are you serious? Why would you do that?"

Jonas stared at Erik, his eyes reflecting deep sadness. "Because if we don't get something going now, I don't think we're ever going to perform together again. That's why."

"Come on, Jonas, don't say that," Erik cajoled. "We agreed to take a year off to get our mojo back. It's only been a couple of months. Give the guys some slack. They need some time off to recharge. We all do."

Jonas lay back with a deep sigh and stared up at the beige canopy overhead. "I don't know if I can last a year. I'll go stir-crazy. A guy can only watch so much TV or play pool."

"Hey," Erik said with a chuckle and reached out, squeezing Jonas's shoulder. "You need a girlfriend. Someone to keep you busy."

Jonas rolled his eyes at the suggestion that a woman would solve all his long-term problems. "Thing is, I need to get back to making music." He stared hard at Erik. "Talk to Alex about recording another album and setting up a world tour to promote it. He'll listen to you. If he's in favor of it, I'll hang on. If he trashes the idea, then I'm out of here."

Erik didn't know what to say. He and Jonas had been friends all their lives. All the guys in the band had known each other since birth. Jonas was a year younger than the rest of the group, but the other members had started kindergarten together and graduated together. The thought of someone leaving the band was inconceivable to him. Losing Jonas would be akin to losing a member of his family.

Sure, they'd had disagreements in the past and in the heat of the moment had thrown around the idea of breaking up, but it was just a way to blow off steam. No one had ever intended to go through with it.

Until now.

Erik stared at his Coke feeling the pressure of being caught in the middle. Alex had only been married a month. No way would he even consider going back to work yet. When Alex said no to the idea, Jonas would split. He had to figure out a way to keep everyone happy, but how?

At this point, he didn't have a clue.

# Chapter Two

### Early October

Clutching a shredded tissue, Carly stood at the edge of the schoolyard, peering through the tall lilac bushes at the kids enjoying the fresh air during recess on the playground. She dabbed at her eyes as she watched a group of fourth graders of the West Loon Bay elementary school chasing each other in a game of tag. Others climbed up the slide, laughing and screaming with delight on the way down. Though she knew all the kids by name, only one child had truly captured her attention. And her heart. A young girl, tall for nine years of age, with reddish-brown hair and deep blue eyes. Rylee Larsen, the child she'd given up for adoption over nine years ago.

She tried to blink away her grief, but a large tear defied her best intentions and spilled from her eye, sliding down her cheek. *If only I had listened to my heart instead of my parents,* she thought miserably, *I wouldn't be here now, hiding like a criminal to get a glimpse of my baby!*

She reached into her shoulder bag and pulled out a fresh tissue. For months, she'd been going over the facts in her mind, torturing herself for the mistakes she'd made as a teen and how she should have done things differently.

*It doesn't any good to relive the past,* she thought as fresh tears rushed to her eyes, *but I can't help it. I should never have given my child away!*

For years, she'd accepted the decision she'd made under duress and believed she'd done the right thing by allowing her cousin, Edith Larsen to take permanent custody of her daughter, Rylee. Edith and her husband, Frank, couldn't have children and were thrilled at the idea of adopting the child. At the time, Edith and Frank had lived in Minneapolis, so it was easy to keep both the baby and the adoption secret. After Frank passed away, however, Edith moved back to West Loon Bay and frequently crossed paths with Carly. She was friendly at first. Then, suddenly, she became fiercely protective of her child.

That was when the heartache started.

Each time Carly ran into Edith and Rylee, the guilt of giving up her child grew until it developed into a full-blown crisis. She couldn't stop thinking about Rylee and waited anxiously to catch a glimpse of her around town. Eventually, she began inventing excuses to visit Edith or show up at functions that they attended—like church and school. Edith caught on to what Carly was doing and, fearing Carly intended to tell Rylee the truth, ended all contact with a restraining order.

Heavy footsteps approached her from behind. Carly turned to find Chris Peterson, West Loon Bay's only full-time police officer, and a former classmate walking toward her. He was in uniform and approached her with solemn dignity, but his eyes reflected a friend's concern.

"Carly," he said in a manner that came across as stern but not unkind, "what are you doing here, peering through the bushes?"

"Well...I..." Her face flushed, embarrassed at being caught sneaking around in a place where she clearly didn't belong. "I was just..."

Resting his hands on his duty belt, he addressed her with a pointed stare. "You're not supposed to be here. It's violating the conditions of your restraining order."

"I know," she replied with a sob. "I'm sorry, Chris. I don't want to get into any trouble. I'll leave right now."

"Hey, hey, calm down," he said and placed his arm around her shoulder giving it a gentle squeeze. "It's nothing personal, Carly. I'm just doing my job. Chief Wyatt told me to keep an eye on you. It's for your own good."

"I was fine until *he* came back, you know," Carly said becoming upset again. "Every time I see him, I start thinking about the past and—"

"Whoa...*he*?" Chris replied as he walked her to her car. "I don't know who you're talking about, but if someone is harassing you, just let me know and I'll take care of it."

"No, I didn't mean it that way," she said as they reached the gold SUV. "He's not harassing me. He doesn't even know the truth about what happened, and for Rylee's sake, I want it to stay that way."

Chris opened the vehicle door for her and stood next to it, bracing his hand on the top of the frame. "Look, I'm not familiar with the person you're referring to, Carly. I have my suspicions, but frankly, it's none of my business and I prefer to keep it that way. The Chief didn't fill me in on your personal situation. He simply said that my job is to make sure you don't violate the restraining order. So, please, leave here now and don't come back. Next time I'll be forced to do more than just give you a verbal warning."

"I understand," Carly said soberly and slipped into the driver's seat. "I'll stay away. I promise."

Chris shut the car door and backed away. He stood in the middle of the street watching as she drove away.

She motored down to Main Street and parked in front of the bakery wondering if they had any fresh cinnamon rolls left. She needed strong coffee and something sweet—and a lot of it. It was only two o'clock in the afternoon, but exhaustion had already set in.

Leaning back in her seat, she exhaled a deep breath as her thoughts traveled back to the scene at the school. Her encounter with Chris had been a close call but it made her realize how utterly obsessed she was with having lost Rylee. Common sense dictated that for everyone's sake—especially Rylee's—she needed to accept her mistake and move on.

*Oh,* she thought desperately, *if only I could!*

"There's no way you're ever going to get Rylee back so stop thinking about it," she said, admonishing herself. "You're torturing yourself over an impossible dream."

Even if she found a lawyer to take on her case, once the public found out, the gossip would destroy Edith's reputation—and hers, but trying to explain the truth to Rylee at this point could upend the child's life. The last thing Carly wanted to do was confuse Rylee and jeopardize her future happiness.

She glanced at the windows of the shops along Main Street, hoping to see a "Help Wanted" sign in one of them. Last month, The Ramblin' Rose bar shut down for good, leaving her unemployed. The owner, Rose Lange, had operated it for twenty-five years, but now that she'd decided to get married to an old flame, the focus of her life had changed, and she no longer wanted to run the business.

With all of the resorts laying off their summer help, fall was a bad time to be unemployed. Carly had moved back home with her parents to cut back on expenses, but she'd been forced to dip into her savings for gas money. If she didn't find a job soon, she'd be broke by Christmas.

From the corner of her eye, she noticed Erik and Alex coming down the sidewalk and heading straight toward her car. Thankfully, they were busy talking and hadn't noticed her yet. Panicking, she slid down in the seat to avoid them, but let out a sigh of relief when they suddenly cut across the street and headed toward the pool hall. In a few moments, they disappeared inside.

Ten years ago, Erik, Alex, and the other members of the band left town without telling anyone. Sadly, because Erik hadn't bothered to pay her the courtesy of saying goodbye, he had no idea what he'd left behind.

No idea at all.

# Chapter Three

## Mid-October

Erik parked his black F-150 pickup under a huge scarlet maple tree and walked down the gravel driveway toward Alex's new double-wide mobile home. Alex and Annika had purchased it for temporary housing on their wooded lot until next summer when the construction of their six-bedroom log home overlooking Lake Tremolo would be completed.

The pungent aroma of sausage pizza wafting through the air filled his nostrils, making his mouth water.

Alex met him at the screen door. "C'mon in. You're just in time for lunch. I made a huge pizza." He looked relaxed today in jeans, a black T-shirt, and stocking feet. His dark wavy hair brushed the back of his neck. The days were still warm, but not warm enough any longer to need air-conditioning.

"I knew what you were making the moment I got out of my car," Erik said with a chuckle. "I wasn't hungry when I got here, but I sure am now.

Alex opened the refrigerator. "Want something to drink? We've got beer, wine, water, and Coke."

"Coke always hits the spot with pizza," Erik replied as he took a seat at the small counter with two barstools. He glanced around at Alex's new digs. The living room, kitchen, and dining area were one large, open room with a vaulted ceiling. "Nice place. You won't have trouble re-selling it once you get the house built."

"Annika has something else in mind for it," Alex said as he opened the refrigerator and pulled out two aluminum cans. "After we move into the new house, we're going to gift it to a local non-profit housing group to place it on a lot in town for a needy family."

"Good call," Erik replied. "Maybe we can get all the guys to donate money for the lot and a garage and make it a group project. We can get our PR people to do a photo op so our fans know we're still alive and kicking."

Alex handed Erik a Coke. "Sure, why not? By the way, Gunnar and Gabe bought adjacent lots down the road. There are only three lots left in this subdivision. If you're looking to build, you'd better hurry up and put some money down on one before they're gone."

"I'm not interested in living so close to the lake. My parents love it," Erik said as he popped the top on his can. "They've got a great view of the lake in the summer and the color in the fall is amazing, but it's not for me. I'm thinking about buying some flat, open land. I want at least forty acres so I can put up a barn and raise a couple of horses. I want to get a dog, too."

Alex laughed as he grabbed his oven mitts. "Man, have you changed! From skin-tight pants, wild hair, and stage makeup to Farmer Brown." He opened the oven and pulled out the hot pizza, placing it on a thick cutting board. "I guess we all have."

Erik placed his Coke on the counter and sat back in his chair. "I'm putting down roots, but that doesn't mean I plan on giving up the record business. Music always will be in my veins. I'm still loyal to the band. The question is, are you?"

Alex's face went blank as though he had no idea what to say.

"What are your plans, Alex?" Erik pressed. "Are you taking a break from the band or are you considering a different future for yourself?"

"We've had a lot of amazing times together. I'm not going to quit," Alex said as he took off the mitts, "but since I just got married five weeks ago, I haven't really thought that far ahead." Pulling open a drawer, he grabbed the pizza cutter and began to slice the pie. "What's with the twenty questions? And why now? We all agreed to take a year off. This is a discussion for next summer, not today."

"You're right," Erik said with a sigh, "and I really don't even feel like having this conversation right now. I've been putting it off, but Jonas is pressuring me."

Alex placed the pizza cutter in the sink. "Why?"

Erik's chest tightened. He didn't like the response he was about to give Alex, but he had to say it. "Jonas wants a guarantee that we're staying together and planning to produce more music or he's going to walk."

"Aren't his demands a little premature? What does he want," Alex asked sarcastically as he opened an upper cabinet and took out two plates, "a world tour?"

Erik shifted uncomfortably in his chair and cleared his throat. "That's exactly what he wants."

"He doesn't call the shots in this band," Alex declared as he set down the plates with a clatter. "You and I do! I don't know about you, but I'm not letting anyone tell me how to run my business. We'll go on tour when *we* say the band goes and that won't be until we're ready. All of us need to agree and be committed to making it work before we start booking venues."

"We need to have a new album in the works before we get to the tour stage," Erik said, correcting him, "but I agree. I didn't make any promises to him. I merely consented to relay the information to you.

Frankly, making plans to go back on the road is the last thing on my mind right now. I want to spend as much time with my dad as I can to make up for the years we've lost."

*And Carly, too,* he thought, wondering if they would ever be friends again or if he was simply fooling himself. He looked away so that Alex, who always seemed to know what he was thinking, couldn't read his thoughts. Right now, they were all about trying to get through that wall of armor that Carly had built around herself.

"Not a word of this to Annika, okay?" Alex asked as he nervously glanced down the short hallway to the bedrooms. "When the time comes, I'll talk to her. She'll get very upset if she hears a rumor and thinks I'm making plans without telling her first. I've promised her a year of no commitments so we can spend every day together and believe me, she will hold me to it."

Erik hadn't seen his sister since he walked in the door, but there were two purses piled on the sofa. "Speaking of Annika, where is she?"

Alex pointed toward a closed door. "She's in the bedroom with Carly. They've been in there ever since they came back from lunch." He shrugged. "They're having another one of their secret *girl* talks."

Erik chuckled at Alex's frustration at being left out of the conversation. "Those two have always done that. Back when they were in middle school, they used to drive me nuts with their whispering and giggling. Where is Carly's car? I didn't see it when I drove up."

Alex grabbed the roll of paper towels and ripped off a couple of sheets for them to use instead of napkins. He pulled the pizza slices apart to cool them faster and picked up one. "Annika was uptown when they ran into each other, so she drove Carly out here to see the house." He bit into his pizza, sucking in air at the same time to cool it in his mouth. "Man, this is good. I'm glad the girls already had lunch. All the more for us!"

Erik grabbed a slice and took a bite of steaming pizza. *Yep.*

He wondered how long the girls would be engrossed in their gossip this time. No matter. When they emerged from the bedroom he would be waiting. This was the first chance he'd had to talk to Carly since the wedding and he had to make it work.

He might never get the chance again.

# Chapter Four

Carly stretched out on Annika's bed and yawned loudly. "Thanks for buying lunch today, but I think I had too much to eat. I'm super sleepy now."

"You'd better not fall asleep on me, girl," Annika said, pretending to be mad. "You'll miss the surprise I've been telling you about."

"Okay," Carly replied as she sat up and fluffed the pillows. "I'm ready. What is it? Are you getting that French bulldog puppy you wanted?"

Annika shook her long, ice-blonde hair. "Nope, Alex says I have to wait on a puppy until next spring. The weather is going to start turning cold in a couple of weeks and it will be a pain to take it outside in the snow a bazillion times a day to potty train it." She smiled mischievously. "This is a lot more exciting anyway. Now close your eyes."

"Close my eyes," Carly repeated. Her jaw dropped. "Wait—are you giving *me* a gift?"

Annika backed against the dresser. "Not exactly, but I guess in a way, you could call it that. Close your eyes. You can't open them until I count to three."

Carly placed a pillow in front of her face so she couldn't peek.

"I'm ready."

"One, two," Annika said as she pulled open a dresser drawer. "Three!"

Carly pushed the pillow away from her face and stared at Annika in confusion. "What?"

Annika held out a long blue and white plastic tube. "Look at this and tell me what it says."

Carly gingerly took the tube. "Is this what I think it is…?" She held up the tube and read the small indicator screen. "Pregnant…3 plus weeks. Oh, my gosh!"

"Yes," Annika said, beaming. "I'm pregnant!"

Carly hugged her squealing with delight. "I'm going to be an auntie!!"

Annika laughed. "Godmother too."

"Hey, what's going on in there?" Alex shouted from the kitchen. "You girls sound like you're having too much fun!"

They burst out laughing.

"Oops!" Annika whispered. "We'd better keep our voices down. Alex doesn't know yet."

Carly stared at Annika in shock. "Are you kidding me? You told me before you broke the news to your husband? Annika!"

"I know, I know," Annika said with a thread of guilt in her voice, "but I just couldn't keep it to myself any longer. Besides, you're my BFF and best friends don't keep secrets from each other!"

Carly's stomach twisted over the secret she'd been keeping from Annika. For years, she'd desperately wanted to confide in Annika about Rylee but couldn't go back on her promise to her parents and Edith to protect Rylee's identity. If word got out, Edith would be devastated, but the damage to Rylee would be even worse. Trying to explain the truth to Rylee about her birth at this point could turn her life upside down. The last thing Carly wanted to do was to hurt Rylee by filling her with confusion and uncertainty.

Annika moved toward the door and opened it a half-inch, peering at the kitchen. "Erik is here. He and Alex are having pizza." She shut the door and turned around. "I performed the test this morning. I was so excited that I drove uptown looking for Alex because he wasn't answering his phone. I was driving down Main Street and saw you when he called me back. He'd just gotten home, and he said that Erik was coming over to talk to him about something important. I was disappointed, of course, but the last thing I wanted was to tell him over the phone, so I decided I'd wait until later today when we're alone."

"He's going to be so happy," Carly said struggling to hide the sadness of her own experience with motherhood. "I'm thrilled for you both."

This was a special time for Annika and Alex and she was truly happy for them. Sadly, her pregnancy had been filled with stress and discord. Once her parents found out about her condition—and that the father had deserted her—they were adamant that the best thing she could do for Rylee was to place the child with Edith and Frank.

"You look so sad," Annika said and slid her arms around Carly. "Don't worry, one of these days it will be your turn to surprise me."

Carly responded with a wry chuckle. "I need to get married first." No way was she *ever* going through pregnancy and childbirth alone again.

They were startled by a knock on the door. Alex stuck his head inside the bedroom. "Come on you two. Erik is here, and he wants to see you, Annika."

"Okay," Annika said as she walked to the door and kissed him. "Give us five minutes."

Alex nodded and shut the door.

"Look, I know how you feel about my brother," Annika said to Carly as she leaned against the door. "I don't understand what's going on between you two, but I don't want to make everybody uncomfortable, so I'll tell him I have to take you home and we'll leave."

Before Carly could respond, Annika opened the door and burst into the kitchen. "Hi!" she said happily to Erik as she hugged him. He wore olive green Dockers today and a camo T-shirt.

Seeing Erik again brought back vivid memories of the night she'd danced in his arms at the wedding. Remembering their conversation and how he'd suggested he still cared for her made Carly's heart skip a beat, but she quickly shoved the thought away. She hadn't believed it then and she still didn't believe it now. It just didn't make sense. If Erik had truly cared so much, why had he cut off all ties with her for a decade?

"Hey, Carly and I were just leaving," Annika said to Erik. "I have to give her a ride back to her car in town. Are you going to be here for a while? I'll be back in ten minutes."

Carly grabbed her purse off the sofa and silently moved toward the front door hoping to make a quick exit. She didn't look up, but her breath caught in her throat as she sensed the intensity of Erik's gaze focused on her.

"I'm leaving anyway," Erik said quickly and stood up. "I can take you back into town."

"Oh, that won't be necessary," she argued grabbing the doorknob. "I wouldn't want to put you to any trouble. Annika can run me back—"

"It's no trouble," Erik insisted as he pulled his keys from his pocket. "I'm going in that direction anyway."

Alex slid his arm around Annika and smiled. "That's great. Thanks! Annika has something she wants to talk to me about."

"I do?" Annika stared at him, flummoxed. "Alex, how did you—"

He squeezed her shoulder and frowned, silencing her.

Jingling his keys, Erik approached Carly. "Shall we go?" Though he sounded confident, uncertainty clouded his deep blue eyes.

Now that Alex had put her on the spot, what else could she do? "Um...sure." Disappointed, she stepped away from the door as Erik reached out to open it for her.

He walked her to his truck in silence and opened the passenger door. She slid in and fastened her seatbelt, setting her purse on her lap. It wasn't much, but it served as a small barrier between them, hopefully discouraging him from getting too close.

"Nice truck," she told him as he slid into the driver's seat and shut the door. "It's huge."

"Thanks. It was a special order." He pulled his seatbelt across his broad chest and snapped it into place. "I picked it up from the dealer last week."

Carly glanced around. The super cab pickup had a large back seat and plenty of room in the front seat. "I can tell. It still has that new vehicle smell."

*And the deep aroma of your cologne*, she thought to herself.

Erik backed out and drove down Alex's long and winding, wooded driveway, bursting with a variety of trees in orange, red and golden leaves. "How have you been, Carly?" He hesitated a few moments as though gauging whether he should continue. "I haven't seen you since the wedding."

"I—I've been busy," she replied a little too quickly, showing her nervousness.

A huge buck darted out from the trees and shot across the road. Erik slammed on his brakes and reached out, bracing his right arm in front of her to prevent her from lurching forward. He had an assortment of tattoos along his arm but one, in particular, caught her attention. The tattoo on his forearm that stood out to her was a heart with a dagger through it. On each side of the dagger, someone had tattooed an initial— C and S respectively.

She couldn't believe her eyes. Were the letters on the tattoo hers or did they belong to someone else with the same initials? Regardless, what did it represent?

*It's none of my business, who he wants to showcase in the ink on his arm*, she thought carelessly. She was better off not knowing. It would save her embarrassment when it turned out to be someone else.

She looked away, acting like she hadn't seen it.

# Chapter Five

The sight of that huge buck leaping in front of Erik's brand-new truck manifested his greatest nightmare. He guessed the rack on that deer to be ten points. The kill would amount to a lot of fresh meat in his dad's freezer, but not this way! Not if he could help it!

"Erik! Look out!" Carly screamed.

He slammed on the brakes and the truck swerved, sliding sideways. The buck sprang out of the way just in time and disappeared into the woods. At the same time, Erik's arm instinctively shot out, bracing against Carly to safeguard her against a possible impact.

His reaction unfolded in a split second, but even so, he caught a glimpse of the shocked look on her face and knew she'd seen the tat. Would she ask about it? He had no idea. If she didn't mention it, he'd let it go. But if she did, he'd tell her the truth.

"That was a close call," he said breathing heavily from the shock. "Grown men don't cry, but if that buck had slammed into my new truck…"

Though it wasn't funny, they burst out laughing to relieve their stress.

Carly sat back, still gasping for breath. "It's how my best friend,

Hope, died last year. The buck that hit her little car demolished the entire front killing her instantly."

"Gosh, I'm sorry to hear that," Erik replied solemnly.

She left his remark unanswered and sat in silence for the rest of the trip.

"Where are you parked?" he asked as he approached Main Street.

"Over by the park," Carly answered. "I always leave my SUV there and walk uptown because it's shady and unlike Main Street, there are plenty of open spaces."

To his surprise, the streets surrounding the park were filled with townspeople. In the bandshell, a local country band played a rousing tune.

"It looks like I'm not going to get anywhere close," Erik said as he slowed the truck to a crawl."

Clutching her purse, she placed her free hand on the door handle. "You can drop me off here. I'll walk the rest of the way."

Even driving slowly, the trip had ended much too soon. He couldn't let her go yet. Gripping his fingers on the wheel, he turned to her with a smile. "Why don't you stick around and listen to the band with me for a while? I've never heard of these guys, and they sound pretty good."

She hesitated, giving him hope. "Well, I..."

"Aw, c'mon. It's a nice fall day and a great way to spend the afternoon."

She frowned at his insistence. "Erik, your band doesn't play country tunes. You're a rocker."

"That doesn't mean I can't appreciate other kinds of music," he countered with a laugh. "I'll bet this band used to play at The Ramblin' Rose, didn't they? You must know them personally."

"Yeah," she said with a nod. "I know them well. They're really nice guys."

"Okay, great! You can introduce me to them. What do you say?"

"I guess so," she replied with a shrug. "I'm sure they'd love to meet you."

Erik found an out-of-the-way parking spot a few blocks from the park, and they walked over to the bandshell to meet the members of Calico Run. The band recognized Carly and Erik right away and when they ended their set, they descended from the stage to meet with the couple. As Carly had stated, the band members were friendly and invited Erik to their next gig at a bar in Summerville. They teased Carly for being a "woofer," the name that diehard fans of Erik's rock band, Wolfmoon, called themselves.

The guys in Calico Run gave them a couple of padded lawn chairs to watch the rest of the concert in comfort. When the concert ended, the crowd began to leave the park. Carly grabbed her purse and stood. "I should go."

The afternoon had passed too quickly for Erik. They hadn't had much to say to each other, but just spending time with her was enough for now. "I'll walk you to your car," he said as he stood. She didn't object, giving him hope that he could see her again. He waved goodbye to the band and thanked them for the chairs.

As they stepped into the street, a young girl with long, reddish-brown hair flew by them on her bicycle, nearly crashing into them. He jumped backward, pulling Carly with him in time to avoid a collision. Something about her looked vaguely familiar but Erik couldn't place what it was that had triggered his curiosity.

"Rylee Jo!!" The shout was a woman's voice. "Get back here and be careful! You almost knocked those people down!"

A half block away, Edith Larsen emerged from a crowd of people.

The short, stout woman wearing black slacks and a flowered blouse marched toward them, glaring at them as soon as she recognized Carly. Her short gray hair and large square glasses made her look much older than the last time he'd seen her, but there was no mistaking her deep, commanding tone.

The little girl called Rylee circled back on her bicycle, pedaling recklessly.

"Rylee, please slow down," Carly said with a cautious thread in her voice, but at the same time, keeping an eye on Edith's reaction.

*What's up with these two*, Erik thought curiously, noting the silent friction passing between the women. *Aren't they related? Why are they staring daggers at each other?*

"Carly!" Rylee shouted as she made a beeline toward them. "Watch this!" She tried to attempt a wheely but when she lifted the front of her bike, she went too high. She lost her balance and crashed to the ground, pinning one of her legs underneath it. Instantly, she began to wail.

A chorus of gasps rose from the crowd as a half-dozen people ran toward the little girl to check on her condition. Carly got there first.

"Rylee, are you okay?" Carly asked, her voice shaking with fear. "Did you hurt your leg?"

Erik gently pulled the bicycle off the little girl hoping she hadn't broken or sprained anything. "There you go," he said and rolled it out of the way. "Can you stand up, sweetheart?"

"I think so," Rylee replied with a sob, rubbing her scraped knee.

Carly knelt next to the little girl, extending her hand. "Let me help you up."

"Get away from her!" Edith screamed at Carly, grabbing her by the arm and pulling her away from Rylee. "You caused this!" She collapsed on the ground next to her child and placed her palm on her forehead as though struggling with dizziness. "Leave my daughter alone!"

Carly stood up; her face paled with shock as she backed away. "No, that's not true! I'd never—"

"It's okay, Carly," Erik whispered in her ear. "I don't know what's wrong with Edith, but she's overreacting."

Carly's large brown eyes filled with tears. "I didn't mean to cause Rylee any harm, I swear."

"You didn't," Erik replied. "You're not to blame."

Edith looked up. Her cheeks were scarlet with anger. "You were warned about this," she whispered. "What's it going to take to make you comply with the order? Don't make me take you back to court, Carly. I guarantee, this time there will be consequences."

"Look, I didn't mean to bother you. Either of you. I'm sorry, but I didn't do anything wrong," Carly argued as her voice broke.

Erik had no idea what they were talking about, but he sensed that Edith truly meant to follow through with her threat. "I think we'd better go," he murmured in Carly's ear and slid his arm around her waist, coaxing her to leave before Edith called the police.

She allowed him to guide her to her SUV, crying silent tears all the way. He wanted to console her, but he didn't understand what was wrong. The scene he'd witnessed didn't make sense to him. Why would Edith adamantly oppose Carly's presence around Rylee? So much that she threatened to take Carly to court?

At her car, he opened the driver's side door. "You're too upset to drive. You need to calm down before you leave here. I'm going to sit with you for a while."

*And I'm not leaving until we talk this out,* he thought with determination.

Once they were both in the car, he sat quietly, debating how to broach the subject. "It's not my place to stick my nose in your business," he said after a few moments, "but I'm concerned about what went down between you and your cousin. If you'd like to talk about it, I'm more than ready to listen."

Her only reply was a burst of sobs.

He opened the glove compartment looking for a tissue and found a travel-sized package. "I want to help you in any way I can," he said with a sense of urgency as he pulled out one and dabbed her cheeks, "but I don't know how to do that unless you tell me what's wrong."

She took the wadded-up tissue from him and blotted her eyes. "I've made a lot of mistakes in my life, Erik," she said with a loud sniffle. "I'm afraid that if I tell you about the most serious one, I'll be making the worst mistake ever. Once you learn the truth, there is no way to undo it."

What mistake? What truth? This was driving him crazy. What was she afraid of? He desperately wanted to know what she was holding back. Because whatever it was, it concerned *him*.

"Look at me," he said gently as he cupped her cheek with his hand. He gazed deeply into her beautiful brown eyes spilling over with lonely, distraught tears. "I know it's too little, too late, but I need to say this. I'm sorry I hurt you, Carly. I should have told you that I was going on the road with Alex. What I did to you was wrong, and I don't blame you for not forgiving me. You have no idea how much I've regretted it all these years. How many times I've longed for this moment to make things right between us."

"Then why," she whispered, "why did you betray me like that?"

He exhaled a deep breath, dreading what he was about to say. "I didn't have any choice. Your dad threatened me. He said he'd kill me if I ever touched you again."

"What?" She sat up straight, blinking in shock. "He said *that*? When?"

"It was after he caught us together in my van. He came to the café the next day when I was working in the kitchen and threatened me in front of my parents. I wasn't afraid of him," he said with a shrug. "I'm a big guy. One punch and he'd—" He sighed, not wanting to go there. Dan Strand was no match for him, but he'd never hurt Carly's dad. "I didn't want to cause any trouble for you, so I agreed to leave you alone."

"I had no idea," Carly said sounding bewildered. "You should have told me."

He shook his head. "It would have only made things worse. I was the one who deserved his wrath. Not you."

She laughed softly, but there was no mistaking the profound sadness in her response. "You have no idea what I went through after that."

"Oh, Carly," he said sincerely. It hurt him to know she had suffered because of him. "I wish I would have known. I would have tried to spare you from it."

"Well, you didn't know, Erik, and it's no use beating yourself up over it now." She stared through the windshield with a wistful look on her face. After a few moments, she said, "They say things happen for a reason, that all things work together for our good, but I don't know what good has come out of this."

There she went again, alluding to something so sad it had robbed her of her joy. She used to be fun-loving and carefree. She loved to laugh. Something terribly tragic had beaten her down.

"Hey," he said, determined to find out. "Tell me about this terrible secret that's tearing you apart, Carly. I want to help you. Whatever happened to you after I left is on me, so I want to fix it, but I can't if I don't know what I did."

41

She looked him in the eyes, her grave expression reflecting a mixture of fear and determination. "You got me pregnant, Erik. Seven months after you left, I gave birth to your baby."

# Chapter Six

The silence in Carly's SUV was deafening. She'd crossed a line with Erik by telling him about Rylee and there was no going back. At the same time, however, she'd burned a serious bridge with not only Edith but her parents as well. The damage had been done but somehow, she didn't feel guilty for breaking her promise to them. Instead, confessing the truth to Erik had liberated her by lifting a burden that had weighed her down for ten years.

Erik's face paled as he absorbed the news. "You mean…" His blue eyes widened in shock. "I'm… a father…?" He sucked in a deep rush of air, as though he'd been holding his breath. "Was that…that little girl of Edith's the one… I mean, is she mine?"

Carly nodded, sympathizing with his confusion. "I'm surprised you didn't notice the resemblance. She's a dead ringer for you, Erik. Her hair is reddish-brown and thicker than mine. Her eyes are as blue as Lake Tremolo on a sunny day. She's got your chin."

"She looked familiar, but I didn't make the connection because I had no reason to suspect we were related," Erik stated. He sat quietly for a while as though he found the unexpected news overwhelming. "What's going on between you and Edith? Why is she so hostile to you?"

"She thinks I'm stalking Rylee." Carly stared down at her hands, unable to hide her guilt. "I…sometimes park by her school and watch her play at recess. Edith found out and filed a restraining order against me to keep me away from her."

"She's afraid someone is going to connect the dots and start spreading rumors."

Carly looked up. "The only reason the whole town isn't already gossiping about Rylee being your love child is that Edith and Frank lived in Minneapolis when she was born. I stayed with them while I was pregnant and had her in a hospital there. Everyone believes she is their daughter."

"I don't understand," Erik said, becoming upset. "Why didn't you try to contact me? Why did you just give up and give her away?"

"Well, for starters," Carly replied crisply, "no one knew where you and the band were for several years. Once you guys became famous, your security was so tight that no one could get near you. Or get your phone number. By that time, it was too late anyway."

Erik wiped a sheen of sweat off his brow and opened the car door a few inches. A rush of refreshing cool air filled the car. "Man, if I'd only known…"

"Well, you didn't, and I was left to make the decisions regarding Rylee's future by myself." She turned in her seat, facing him. "Look, I didn't want to let her go. I swear! Releasing her for adoption was the most heart-wrenching decision I've ever had to make. You have no idea how difficult it was for me to sign the papers giving away my parental rights and how much I've agonized over it since then. At the time, I had no alternative and because of that, my parents pressured me to go through with it."

He pushed the door open wider. "How could Dan and Darla turn their backs on their own grandchild?"

"I know it sounds heartless," Carly said solemnly, "but you know how mean-spirited some of the people in this town can be. They gossip mercilessly about everybody. Even if I had eventually married and my husband had agreed to adopt Rylee, everyone would still look upon her as an illegitimate child. My parents went through some difficult soul-searching over it, but in the end, they believed it would be best for her if Edith and Frank raised her as their own."

Tipping his head back, he sighed and stared at the ceiling, mulling over the situation. "I didn't sign any papers. And I didn't make any promises to anyone. What if I want my child to know who her real father is?"

"That's a major problem, Erik," Carly said, knowing she had to reason with him on this point. "It's the same issue I've been dealing with ever since Frank died and Edith moved back to West Loon Bay. Nothing is stopping me from telling Rylee the truth, but once the cat is out of *that* bag, there's no getting it back in. Rylee believes Edith is her mother and Frank was her dad. What would happen to her emotional state if she found out that everything she believed in was a lie? You can't breathe a word of this to anybody!"

He gave her a long, serious look. "I guess you're right about that. I'm sure it would be very difficult for her as a child to understand the situation. Just the same, ignoring the problem isn't going to make it go away. Eventually, she'll become an adult, and if she decides to get a DNA test, she's going to find a few surprises in her family tree. What I'm trying to say, Carly is that your secret isn't really safe. Someday the truth is going to come out. Unfortunately, there is no easy solution to the problem."

"No, there isn't," she said sadly. "So, we're back to where we started."

"What about us?" He twined his fingers around hers. "Can we go back to where we started?"

Her heart began to flutter but her head warned her to resist him with all her might. "I don't think that would be a good idea." She pulled her hand away. "We're not the same people we were a decade ago."

"No, we're not, but maybe that's a good thing," he replied with enthusiasm. "We're not the impetuous kids we once were. We've both been through some stuff, and it has matured us. Made us stronger people."

"Yeah, well, some of us have no idea what it's like to go from rags to riches," Carly shot back.

He responded with a wry laugh. "Believe me, ten years on the road wasn't the dream life everyone thinks it was. Our lives were glamorized in pictures to sell magazines, but the truth is we were constantly traveling and performing on fast food and little sleep."

She shot him a glare to demonstrate her disbelief. "Don't tell me you didn't enjoy the wild parties and all of the glamorous women hanging all over you."

"I'm not going to lie. Of course, I did," he confessed, "and for years, I couldn't get enough of it. All of it. I thought I was on top of the world but in reality, my life consisted of hangovers and fatigue, and drugs to prop me up. Eventually, I realized what an empty existence I'd created for myself. We all did. That's why we came home. We desperately needed to take some time off and reevaluate our lives."

"Until you get tired of living in the sticks," Carly said and looked away, realizing how dull and simple her life had been compared to his. He was a millionaire looking to escape a life of self-destruction. She was an unemployed nobody looking for a job. She knew what he wanted, but she had no interest in serving as temporary entertainment for his extended vacation. "Then you'll be gone again. Looking for a new adventure."

"That's not true," Erik argued. "West Loon Bay is my home. I came back to stay." He shut the car door and moved close, looking deeply into her eyes. "Everything I cherish is here."

Before she had a chance to pull away, he slid his palm around the back of her neck and drew her close as his mouth covered hers, brushing her lips with a gentle caress. She froze at first, then instantly, it all came back; the taste of his lips on hers, the heat of his arms around her, the melding of their body chemistry—everything they'd shared when they were younger and were ruled by their passions. A still, small voice in her head warned her to resist, but she ignored it and slid her arms around his neck, leaning into his kiss as an ache buried deep in her soul awakened, intensifying with each beat of her heart.

He deepened his kiss and possessively encircled his arms around her waist, pulling her close in a confident way that demonstrated his years of experience. As she pressed against his chest, their hearts began to beat in sync. Her breath grew shallower and faster as his hand slid up her back.

*Be careful,* her thoughts screamed. *Is this what you really want to happen? You know where this is leading.* Her mind raced as her emotions swirled with doubt. *Yes! No! I don't know...*

Once upon a time, she had loved him so much that she would have given up everything in a heartbeat for him if he'd asked her. But he didn't. Instead, he gave her up to pursue a new life, hurting her more than he would ever know. Capitulating to his desire for her now would expose her to the same hurt and humiliation she'd suffered only this time she knew better. This time she had the advantage of having been down this road before and she knew what waited for her at the end.

She pulled away, breathless from the toll his eagerness had taken on her self-control. The flame between them had lit too fast and would burn out of control unless one of them used some common sense. "Erik, no. Stop—I can't."

"Why?" Taking deep breaths, he slowly released his grip, letting her know how reluctant he was to let go of her. "What's wrong?"

Shaking, she sat back in her seat and straightened her shirt. "This isn't a good idea. One moment we're talking. The next moment we're all over each other. Things are happening too fast."

"We're not kids any longer, Carly," he said. "We know what we're doing. I know you care for me as much as I care for you."

She needed to leave before he talked her into agreeing to something she knew she'd regret later. "That's my point, Erik. A lot has happened since the last time we were together. We have a lot to work through before we get involved again. *If* we ever get involved again that is. I think we should leave things as they are. At least, for now."

"Please don't shut me out," Erik said with an urgent plea in his voice. "We can make it work this time. I know I don't deserve it, but I'm asking for a chance to make things right."

Oh, how she desperately wanted to believe him! "I don't know if I could ever trust anyone again much less you, Erik."

"We'll take things one day at a time," he whispered in her ear. "I promise, I won't leave you again. You and Rylee."

She looked down at the tattoo on his forearm bearing her initials. "What does this mean?"

"I got it not long after we went on the road," he said. "I didn't have anyone to talk with about it and I needed to express my feelings. What it means is leaving you without saying goodbye pierced like a dagger through my heart."

A sob caught in her throat. *Oh, if he only knew...*

# Chapter Seven

## October 31st

"Trick or treat!"

Erik pulled back the sheer curtain and stared out the living room window as his short, gray-haired mother, Helen, stood on the front porch in the cool evening air, handing out miniature candy bars to a couple of excited elementary school children. The sun had barely set when kids of all ages began to show up at the door in an assortment of colorful costumes and chanting their favorite mantra.

Earlier, Gunnar had called and wanted Erik to meet him and Gabe for dinner in Summerville, but Erik had to pass, having promised Helen that he would help her decorate and greet the trick-or-treaters tonight. Later, after the candy was gone and the little goblins were home in bed, he planned to meet the guys at a bar for a few rounds of Halloween cheer.

"Erik, I need another bag of Snickers," Helen said as she shut the screen door. She gave him a wry grin. "And this time, don't eat half of them." They laughed. Both had been sampling the goods ever since they pulled out the candy bowl.

He went into the family room where his father lay stretched out on the sofa. Knut was supposed to be watching the Vikings football game—at least that was his excuse for not handing out candy—but his snoring sounded like a foghorn, drowning out the raucous cheers coming from the television. The Vikings were playing the Packers tonight. All day, giddy with nervous anticipation, Knut had talked non-stop about how the Vikings were favored to win by one point. As a Minnesotan, losing to Wisconsin—or the Cheeseheads, as Minnesotans called them—was a fate worse than death.

Chuckling, Erik grabbed several bags of candy bars and closed the door on his way out.

Earlier that day, Helen had recruited him to help her set up the wraparound porch on their large Victorian home with miniature bales of hay, carved pumpkins, paper skeletons, and stretchy spiderwebs. Luminaries of orange paper bags with bat cutouts lined the front sidewalk.

He hadn't celebrated Halloween the old-fashioned way since he left home and had forgotten how festive the evening could be. Back when he was a kid, Helen and Knut's lake home, located at the edge of town, typically got a lot of elementary kids on foot before the sun went down. After dark, the older kids showed up in groups. Some rode in the bed of a pickup or a hay wagon pulled by a tractor. Others sat on a snowmobile trailer pulled by a pickup or a large ATV.

He wondered what Carly was doing at this moment. Was she decorating her mother's porch and handing out candy? Waiting for the bigger kids to show up looking like zombies, Freddie Kruger or Jason Voorhees? Ever since that night in the park, he'd called her every morning to stay in touch and let her know he was thinking of her. She'd received his calls warily at first, but with each passing day, their conversations grew longer and filled with laughter as their friendship deepened.

"What do you think of my Star Wars costume," Helen said proudly as she spun around showing off a full-length garment with a pointed tail that dragged on the floor. It had a beige front, dark brown on the back with dark brown sleeves. "I got it cheap at a garage sale last summer."

She showed him the character's name stitched on the tail.

"Ma, do you have any idea who Jabba the Hutt is?" he replied as he struggled not to laugh. "He's a huge slug-like character that eats frogs. Where is your headpiece?"

She shrugged. "I didn't know it came with one, but it would have been too hot to wear, anyway."

*I'm glad of that,* he thought with relief. If any of his bandmates saw his mother dressing up like a giant gastropod, he'd never hear the end of it.

All of the kids who came to the house were entertaining in their costumes, but Erik enjoyed the littlest ones the most. Dressed as kitties, unicorns, Barney the Dinosaur, or Baby Yoda, they would stand at the door with their miniature pumpkin-style candy buckets and stare silently up at Helen while their parents urged them to say "trick-or-treat" for the candy. No amount of coaxing on her part could get the toddlers to speak. Erik wondered if Rylee had been the same way at that age. Sadly, he would never know.

He'd always wanted to build a home on acreage for privacy, but now that he knew about Rylee, all he wanted was to build it for *her*. He sighed. The possibility of his daughter living under his roof or even spending time with him was about as likely as him rocketing to the moon. An exciting prospect, but not in this lifetime.

Each time the doorbell rang, the possibility of Rylee standing on the other side of the screen crossed his mind. He had no interest in handing out candy, that was Helen's job, but if he saw Rylee, he wanted to be the one to speak to her and fill her bucket with treats. He hadn't stopped thinking about her since the day she fell off her bike at the park and scraped her knee. If she stopped by tonight, he planned to get a good look at his *mini-me* and point out how much he liked her costume as an excuse to speak to her. Well, if he recognized her. Some kids wore full face masks. Hopefully, he would be able to pick her out.

"I ran into Mabel Richardson in the grocery store this morning. She said her neighbor saw you and Carly Strand together in her car the night of the Calico Run concert in the park," Helen announced in her usual direct way. She placed her hands on her square hips. "You were kissing."

*Great,* he thought as his chest tightened. *Did the neighbor overhear our conversation as well?*

"So, I was kissing a girl," he replied offhandedly. "What's wrong with that?"

Helen scowled. "Carly isn't just any girl. She's the town tramp."

"Is that so? Then, what do people call me?" Erik snapped as he walked into the kitchen. He held out a tattoo-covered arm. "The prince of darkness?"

Helen ignored his snarky gesture. "It's just that everybody knows you two have a past so to see you together again..."

"We had a crush on each other in high school," Erik replied with a shrug. "I wouldn't call that much of a past."

"The way it ended generated a lot of salacious gossip," Helen said emphatically as she followed him. "Carly had a bad reputation back then and she didn't improve it by working in that dive Rose Lange calls The Ramblin' Rose. I'm glad that place closed down."

He jerked the refrigerator door open and grabbed a chilled bottle of water. "I don't care what the gossips in this town say about me, but I don't want to hear anything bad about Carly. She's a good person."

"All I'm saying, Erik, is don't get involved with her again. The last thing you need is to get swept into her drama," Helen argued.

He shut the refrigerator door and spun around. "I know you mean well, Ma, but that's up to me to decide."

Helen grabbed his free hand and squeezed it. "I just don't want you to get into another bad situation with that girl. I worry about you."

*Too late*, he thought sadly. *I'm already in too deep.*

The doorbell rang. Helen charged into the front entry and opened the screen door. "Well…" she said sounding excited. "Come on in everybody. Here, grab some candy bars. Erik!"

Curious, Erik hurried to the front door to see who'd arrived.

Jonas stood inside the door with his eight-year-old niece and ten-year-old nephew, Mia and Michael. Mia wore a mermaid costume. Michael was a pirate. Jonas looked stressed.

Erik grinned. "Babysitting tonight?"

"Yeah," Jonas said and shoved his hands into the pocket of his jeans. "My sister and her husband wanted to go to a Halloween party, but she lost her sitter at the last minute." He frowned. "I don't mind hanging out with the little headbangers. We have a blast together, but this is the third time this week I've been conscripted to watch them."

Erik laughed. "Jean owes you big time. Someday when you have kids you can collect. Want a beer?"

"When are we gonna go?' Michael wailed. "I'm bored."

"Nah, thanks anyway," Jonas replied quickly and placed his hand on the door latch. "We still have a lot of ground to cover, and the kids want to visit the park tonight. They've got a haunted house set up there and a hayride." He opened the door and the kids charged outside, running down the sidewalk. "Hey! You guys wait up!" He turned to Erik. "Did Alex give you a straight answer yet about the tour?"

"He's still thinking about it," Erik said, making up a quick lie to buy him some time. He didn't want to get into what Alex *really* said in front of Helen and be subjected to fifty questions when Jonas left. The tour was a subject that the entire group needed to discuss together, but not now. He hoped he could put Jonas off until after the holidays but if push came to shove, he was putting his foot down. No discussion about it until the end of their one-year sabbatical.

Erik went into the family room to watch the football game, hoping Helen had forgotten about Carly for now. She kept busy handing out candy until darkness fell and the younger kids stopped coming.

Around seven o'clock, the doorbell rang.

"Erik, will you get that?" Helen called from somewhere upstairs.

The Vikings were on the verge of making a touchdown. He didn't want to leave the game, but he got up anyway. *Throw the candy into their buckets and get right back to the TV*—that was the plan.

A single child stood on the porch peering through the screen. And there she was, dressed like a princess. Her shiny blue dress fell to her shoe tops in thick folds. Her thick dark hair had been wound into a topknot and adorned with ice blue glitter and a sparkling crown. Someone had painted snowflakes and swirls of glitter on her cheeks.

As he gazed upon her with fascination, the world melted away. Nothing mattered at this moment except the sweet little girl he'd newly discovered was his child. Her wide blue eyes stared up at him with innocence and curiosity. "Trick or treat," she said softly and held up her Halloween bag bulging with candy.

Slowly, he opened the screen door and positioned the special washer on the closer to keep it from shutting again. Grabbing the candy bowl, he knelt to be eye-level with her. "Hey, Rylee," he said in a happy voice as he grabbed several candy bars and dropped them into her bag. "I like your costume. It's beautiful."

"I'm Elsa," she said proudly.

"Okay," he replied, totally unfamiliar with that character. "How's your knee? Is it healing?"

She nodded. "It doesn't hurt anymore."

"That's great. Glad to hear that," he said, anxious to keep the conversation going. "You're pretty good on your bike. Do you ride it a lot?"

"Yeah," she said as her face lit up. "I can go just as fast as the boys in my school!"

*Such a beautiful smile,* he thought. *It's just like Carly's.*

"I'll bet you can," Erik said and dropped more candy into her bag.

"Say thank you so we can get going, Rylee," Edith Larsen called from the sidewalk. "We've still got more houses to visit."

"I gotta go," Rylee said, looking back at Edith. She turned around. "Bye."

Helen came up behind Erik and waved. "Happy Halloween!"

Rylee waved back. "Bye, Helen!" She headed toward the stairs but when she reached them, instead of taking the steps like a little lady, she leaped over them, landing on her feet on the sidewalk with a thud.

"Good job!" Erik burst out laughing. *She's just like me at that age,* he thought proudly. *A rambunctious kid who likes to show off.*

"Don't encourage her," Edith shouted, laughing with him. "Otherwise, she'll keep it up all night!" She adjusted her shoulder strap purse and waved at Helen. "Let's have lunch one of these days. Now that school has started, I have lots of free time."

"Sounds good," Helen called back as Edith walked away. "I'm available almost any day."

Erik loosened the washer on the door closer and stood, stepping back as the door slowly shut. "I didn't know you and Edith were such good friends."

"I've known her for years," Helen remarked. "Back when your father and I ran the café, Edith and Frank used to come for the all-you-can-eat dinner special almost every Friday night. After she and Frank moved to the Twin Cities, I only saw her a couple of times a year, but we stayed in touch."

Erik stood at the screen door watching Edith and Rylee walk to the next house. "So, you know Rylee, too."

"Oh, yes. She's a sweet little girl," Helen said wistfully. "This time next year, Annika's baby will be four months old, and hopefully I'll have my first granddaughter to dress up for Halloween."

*You already do*, Erik thought sadly. *She's been living right under your nose for a long time. You just don't know it.*

Loud cheering echoed from the other room. Darn! Something big had happened in the game, and he'd missed it.

"Edith has filed a restraining order against Carly Strand," Helen said gravely as she filled the candy bowl again.

Stunned, Erik stopped at the family room doorway. His hand gripped the doorknob. "How do you know that?"

"Mabel says Edith let it slip on the night of the concert. She was standing close to Edith and heard her whisper a threat to Carly." Helen set the bowl on a small table by the door. "Edith isn't well, you know. She's been having trouble lately keeping her diabetes under control. She doesn't need problems with Carly Strand, too." She sighed. "I fear things are only going to get worse for poor Edith. The gossip going around town now is that Rylee is Carly's illegitimate child and that's why she won't stay away."

Erik's palms began to sweat. "Is there proof?"

Helen responded with a wry laugh. "People in this town don't care about proof. They saw the way Edith reacted to Carly and that was all the evidence they needed."

He walked toward her, suddenly forgetting about the game. "Who do *they* have pegged as the father?"

"This thing is getting hot," Helen said as she unzipped her costume and began to pull it off.

The way she delayed answering made him nervous. "Ma, who are people saying is the father…"

"It was a long time ago," Helen replied and carefully stepped out of the Star Wars suit. "Carly ran around with different ones, staying out all night and creating a real headache for her parents. She was eighteen by then so there was nothing Dan Strand could do about it. I remember, at the time hearing that they'd shipped her off to the cities to find a job and enroll in a two-year college. People are now wondering if it was to hide a pregnancy."

He drew in a deep breath, growing impatient. "By whom…?"

Helen slipped her suit over a hangar and hung it in the coat closet. "The name that's being tossed around right now is Andy Bradt."

*Andy Bradt?* Erik blinked in shock, unable to see straight. Anderson "Andy" Bradt was his worst enemy in high school. Rivals who delighted in beating each other up after class, Erik had spent many hours in detention for "getting into it" with Andy over the smallest of insults. But this—this was worse than a sucker punch in front of the whole town.

"Andy Bradt is not the father of her kid!" he bellowed.

"Oh, so Rylee *is* her child," Helen said emphatically, verbally salivating over her newest bit of gossip. "I'm guessing she told you that herself. Well, if Andy isn't the father, did she tell you who is?"

"*I am.*"

The words shot out before he could stop himself. The look on his mother's face made his heart pound like a sledgehammer.

*What have I done?*

For once in her life, she didn't have a response. She stared at him wide-eyed through her tortoiseshell glasses, looking like she might faint.

She stumbled into the living room and collapsed onto an armchair.

Upset with himself for telling her the truth, Erik followed her and sat on the sofa. "Look, I wasn't supposed to tell anybody, so you *have to* keep this confidential. Rylee doesn't know that she's adopted and—"

"How long have you known," Helen interjected.

He let out a deep breath. "A couple of weeks. Carly told me at the park, but only after I questioned why Edith threatened her. It made her so upset she could hardly—"

"All these years I've been dying for a grandchild, and I didn't know that I already had one." Helen's eyes filled with angry tears as her fingers gripped the arm of the chair. "Darla did, though, and she could have told me. She *should* have told me, but she withheld it from me on purpose. She denied me the right to know my own granddaughter!"

Erik leaned close, taking her hands in his. "Ma, I know you're upset. You had the right to know. We both did, but the situation isn't that simple. You see, Rylee doesn't know she's adopted, and the Strands believe it would be traumatic for her if the truth came out because she's too young to understand. We need to keep this between me and you. For now. All right?"

Helen pulled her hands away and tossed them upward in disgust. "The Strands! I feel like giving them a good piece of my mind!"

The phone rang.

*Why now?* Frustrated, Erik sat back and stared at the ceiling as Helen grabbed her cordless landline phone off the end table.

"It's Alex," Helen remarked with concern as she stared at the screen. "Why is he calling at this hour? Shouldn't he be watching the game? Or are the Vikings losing to the Packers again?" She put the phone to her ear. "Hello?" She went silent again as she listened to him, her brows furrowing with alarm. "Oh, my God, Alex. No! We'll be right there."

She hung up the phone. "It's Annika. She's in the hospital. There's a problem with the baby," she said, her voice shaking. "I had my first grandchild stolen from me. Now the second one may not survive. Why is God punishing me like this? Start the car, Erik. I'll wake up Knut." She stood up, pointing a warning finger at him. "Not a word about Rylee to your father. All right? There's no use upsetting him now. We've got to get through Annika's crisis first. Then we'll talk again."

Helen walked into the family room and shut off the television.

Erik stood and went to the front closet to get his fleece jacket wondering how such a fun night could go bad so easily. What a mess. His dad always said that things came in threes. What else was about to go wrong?

# Chapter Eight

Carly drove straight to the hospital in Summerville, anxious to get more information about Annika's condition. Alex sounded so distraught when he called her that she cut the conversation short and jumped into the car, deciding it would be best to speak with him in person. The drive to Summerville took twenty minutes—twenty interminable minutes to fret about her best friend's condition.

She grabbed the first spot in the parking lot that she could find, locked her car, and jogged across the blacktop to the front entrance. At the information desk, she inquired about Annika's whereabouts. Was she still in the emergency room? The woman at the desk gave her Annika's location and she took off toward the elevator bank. She didn't slow down until the elevator doors closed and she stood alone in the car.

Oh, how she hated hospitals! They made her uncomfortable in that she would always be reminded of her only visit as a patient—a maternity patient. It wasn't Rylee's birth that bothered her, though. It was the act of handing her baby off to Edith that had caused her so much trauma.

Alex stood in the hallway outside of Annika's room with his mother, Rose Lange, and her fiancé, Hugh Wyatt.

"Calm down, Alex," Rose said, clutching him by the upper arms. "Worrying can't control the outcome. I'm sorry. The doctors can only do so much. Nature will take whatever course it takes. The main thing is that you stay strong for Annika so you can support her through this."

Rose measured at five feet-four-inches, just brushing the edge of Alex's chin but she had the tenacity of a wolf. Blonde and petite, she favored western wear and turquoise accessories. Today she wore knee-length boots, snug-fitting beige jeans, and a suede and lace jacket in beige with a turquoise necklace. She changed her hairdo occasionally, but at the present, she wore it shoulder length and parted it on the side.

Alex looked just like his dad, tall with black hair and brown eyes. He'd learned recently that Hugh Wyatt, Rose's fiancé, was his biological father. For reasons of her own, Rose had kept the secret of Alex's parentage until he was thirty years old. No one knew why, except Alex, and he had never offered an explanation.

"How is Annika," Carly asked Alex, breathless from hurrying. "Can I see her?"

"The nurse is with her right now," he said in a tired voice as he ran his hands through the waves of his thick, kohl hair. His dark eyes were filled with exhaustion and worry. A heavy five o'clock shadow covered his jaw.

"How are you doing?" she asked with concern. "Are you okay?"

"I'm worried about her," Alex replied with a tired sigh, "but there's nothing I can do except walk the floor. I've never felt so helpless in my life."

Down the hall, the elevator doors opened, and Helen charged out of the car, hurrying toward them. Knut trailed behind her. Then Erik.

Their gazes met and held as he walked toward her.

He approached the group, but his attention focused solely on her. Her stomach leaped with apprehension as the words he spoke to her the last time they met flashed through her mind.

We'll take things one day at a time," he whispered in her ear. "I promise, I won't leave you again. You and Rylee."

Could she believe him this time? Could she trust him?

He approached her. "What's going on? Why is everyone standing out here?"

"The nurse is with Annika right now," Carly said quietly. "I just got here myself."

"Where's my daughter?" Helen demanded loudly. "I want to see her!"

The door to Annika's room suddenly opened and a short, dark-haired nurse appeared in lavender scrubs covered with goblins, bats, and pumpkins. "You may see her now."

Helen rushed in first. Everyone waited for Alex to go next.

Carly held back as everyone gathered at the door, crowding into Annika's room. Erik stayed with her and held the door for her.

"I want to see Annika, but this room is way too congested for me," she whispered to him. "It's going to get really stuffy in here."

"How are you doing? Is everything alright?" Helen asked in a thick voice as she approached Annika's bed and took her hand. Alex stood on the other side holding her other hand. "Is there a problem with the baby?"

Annika's face looked pale and drawn. Dark circles underscored her eyes. "I've been spotting all day," she said sounding fatigued. "Alex and I decided that I should come to the hospital and get it checked out. The staff is going to do some tests."

*Oh, my gosh, I hope it isn't serious*, Carly thought anxiously as she clasped her hands together.

"We're all pulling for you, sis," Erik said. "You and the baby."

"You need more rest," Helen announced with the air of a drill sergeant. "When the doctor says you can go home, you're coming to my house to stay. I'll take care of you." She patted Annika's hand. "You and Alex will move into your old room."

Annika exchanged worried glances with Alex. "But Mom—"

"I'm your mother and *I* know what's best," Helen countered stubbornly.

The door opened letting in a rush of cool air as the nurse returned, announcing that Annika's doctor had arrived. Everyone needed to exit the room so he could examine her.

Knowing they had no time to talk, Carly blew her a kiss and turned to leave with the others.

"Carly, wait," Annika called out and motioned for Carly to come to her. "I'm so glad you're here," she said with tears in her eyes as Carly reached her bedside. "This is turning into a circus," she whispered. "Get me out of here."

"You're going to be fine," Carly said in a soft voice to reassure her. "You and the baby." She grabbed Annika's hand and squeezed it. "You'll be out of here before you know it."

"If I get a girl, I'm naming her Hope," Annika said with a sniffle. Ten months ago, their best friend, Hope Cummings had died in a tragic accident, and they'd vowed to always honor her memory.

"Lucky girl," Carly said teasingly. "Of course, you're going to name her Hope if you have a girl. You always beat me to the punch at everything."

They laughed, casting a moment of lightheartedness over a grim situation.

"The doctor's waiting," Erik whispered as he slid his arm around Carly's shoulders and guided her toward the open door where the nurse stood waiting for them to exit.

"Call me later and let me know what the doctor says," Carly called out as she raised her hand to wave farewell. "Bye!"

"Bye, sis," Erik chimed in. "Love ya!"

"Where did everyone go?" Carly asked once they left the room and entered an empty hallway.

Erik glanced around. "They must have gone somewhere to get a cup of coffee." He took her by the hand. "Let's take a walk. We could both use some fresh air." He hesitated. "I need to talk to you about something."

The grave tone in his words gave her pause. "What about?"

He glanced around again. "Not here. Someplace where we can talk privately."

A chill seeped down her spine. Whatever he had to say, he wasn't looking forward to it. "There's a small park next to the building where people go to smoke," she said and zipped up her red fleece hoodie.

They left the hospital and walked to a small area hidden from the parking lot with tall lilac bushes and flower gardens, now all bare. The meditation pond had been drained, but the benches and the decorative lighting remained. They walked around for a little while taking in the peace and quiet and gazing at the starry sky.

"Are you leaving?" Carly asked sharply as she plopped down on a park bench, expecting the worst. "Are you going back to California?" The crisp words billowed from her lips in the chilly evening air in small, misty puffs. "Is that what this is about?"

He stopped abruptly, as though he hadn't expected the question. "No. I told you before that West Loon Bay is my home. I'm here to stay."

She crossed her legs at the knee and folded her arms, bracing herself for bad news. "Then…what's the confession you need to get off your chest?"

"My mom made a statement that upset me and it...I said some things I shouldn't have."

*Wow*, Carly thought. *That must have been some statement.*

A sudden breeze caused her to shiver. She pulled the zipper on her hoodie up to her neck. "What did she say that got you so worked up?"

He sat down beside her, stretching his arm behind her across the backrest of the bench. "She said people have been speculating for years that you went to Minneapolis when you were eighteen to conceal the fact that you were having a baby."

Carly shrugged. "I know there has been gossip about me. Proving it is another matter."

"According to my mother, people in West Loon Bay don't care about proof. If it sounds good, it's gospel." He paused. "That's why when she said the story going around was that Andy Bradt was the father, it ticked me off so much that I...um...might have accidentally admitted to her it wasn't true because Rylee was *my* child."

Her world suddenly fell apart. "What?" She jumped to her feet. "You told Helen about Rylee? Erik, how could you? I shared that with you in confidence!"

He winced at the accusation in her reply. "It—it just came out. When she said you and Andy had—"

"Nothing happened between me and Andy Bradt! Ever! Your mother is gossip central, Erik. Running the only café in town for decades gave her a ringside seat to every tidbit of juicy chatter making the rounds. Her old cronies still pump her for information because they know she couldn't keep a secret if her life depended upon it!"

This time, unfortunately, Rylee's life depended upon it.

"She just found out before we left for the hospital, so she hasn't had time to even break the news to my dad," he said nervously tapping his fingers on the bench. "I'm as worried about this as you are and that's why I'm telling you it happened. What are we going to do?"

"Not we, Erik. You! What are *you* going to do about this? It's your mother. She won't listen to me. She doesn't even like me!"

She stomped away, so angry she could barely control herself. How could he have been so careless? She wanted to slug him!

He sprang from the bench and grabbed her by the arm, pivoting her to face him. "Look, we'll approach her together. You and me. Rylee is *our* child and it's time we joined forces."

Carly swallowed hard, thinking about the ramifications of the information becoming public. "Erik, if she breathes a word of this—"

"She won't," he argued. "I'll make sure of that. I promise." Sliding his palms around her neck, he tilted her chin upwards with his thumbs. "This is a big deal to her. I never realized how much she wanted grandchildren. She started to cry when it sunk in what I'd said because of all the years she'd missed out on spending time with her granddaughter. We'll make her understand how important it is to keep this quiet."

She let out a deep breath. "Okay, but we need to do it *right now.*"

"In a moment…" His gaze dropped to her lips, and when he kissed her, she found it difficult to resist. Deep down, she wanted him to kiss her even though she knew it could lead to more hurt, to breaking her heart again. She'd wanted him to kiss her again ever since the night they went to the concert in the park.

"Rylee may be out of reach, but *we* have each other," he said tenderly as he kissed her. "We can start over, Carly, and this time it'll be different. We're older and wiser. We won't let the mistakes of our past affect our future together."

She buried her cheek in his shoulder, breathing in the scent of his bold cologne, absorbing his gentle strength as he held her. Nothing more needed to be said. The possessiveness of his arms surrounding her gave her the courage to face whatever happened with Helen. They stood together for a while, holding each other as their kisses grew deeper and more fervent.

"We'd better go," he said, reluctantly pulling his arms away. "It's getting late and they're probably wondering what happened to us."

They walked back to the hospital and took the elevator to the second floor. The hallway looked deserted when they arrived. All was quiet on the floor. The door to Annika's room stood partially open. Alex sat in a chair next to her bed, watching television with her.

"What's going on?" Erik asked as they entered the room.

Carly looked at her watch. It was almost eleven o'clock. She had a bad feeling about this. "Where is everybody?"

Annika sighed. "My doctor says everything appears okay with the baby, but he wants to err on the side of caution, so I have to spend the night here for observation. When everybody found out, they went home."

Carly and Erik stared at each other in surprise.

"Helen and Knut didn't know where you were, Erik, and you weren't answering your phone, so they got a ride home from my parents," Alex stated.

"I put my phone on silent when we went for walk," Erik sheepishly replied. "I didn't want to be disturbed."

Carly glanced out into the silent hallway, hoping their presence wasn't disturbing the other patients. "We'd better get going, too. It's late."

Alex rose from his chair and kissed Annika. "I'm really tired. I should be going, as well, but I'll be back first thing tomorrow morning."

The men walked Carly to her car. Erik opened the door for her. "My parents will probably be in bed by the time I get home."

"Yeah, I figured that," Carly replied as she tossed her purse onto the passenger seat and slid in behind the wheel.

Erik rested his hand on the top of the door and leaned in, kissing her goodbye. "I'll talk to her tomorrow," he whispered. "First thing. I promise."

"Okay." She placed her key into the ignition. "It's probably better that you speak to her alone anyway."

"Drive carefully," he said, quoting his parents and hers.

She grinned at him as he shut the door, keeping the humor of that thought to herself. Frankly, it was the only thing she had to smile about.

\* \* \*

November 1st

Annika called Carly at noon the next day to let her know that she'd been released from the hospital but was going to stay with her mother because the doctor advised that she take it easy. Helen had shown up at the hospital early that morning and insisted that Annika come home with her.

Erik called Carly later and verified that he'd had *the talk* with Helen, and she had agreed to keep Rylee's identity confidential.

All seemed well. For now…

Two days later, Annika called Carly at home. "Hey, cowgirl. What are you doing?"

Carly sighed. "I'm on the computer, looking for a job, but I'm not finding anything. What are you doing?"

"Nothing," Annika replied quickly. "I'm bored. This business of resting all day sucks! And my mother is driving me nuts."

"Living with our parents after we've been on our own *is* a challenge," Carly replied with a chuckle. "I'm not used to telling someone where I'm going and when I'll be home. I'll be glad when I get another job and can get my own place again."

"Why don't you come over?" Annika asked. "I'm stuck here all by myself for a few hours. The house is too quiet."

Carly took the news with a pang of disappointment at missing Erik. "Why are you alone? Where did everybody go?"

"Erik and Alex took my dad fishing and Mom is having lunch with Edith Larsen," Annika said. "Then she and Edith are going shopping."

The news about Helen visiting Edith caused Carly's heart to skip a beat. "Edith Larsen?" she asked in a high-pitched voice, giving away her nervousness. She cleared her throat. "Why Edith?"

"They're old friends," Annika replied casually. "Edith and Frank used to eat at the café every week before they moved to Minneapolis. What time are you coming over?"

Carly checked her sports watch. "I have to take a shower first. I'll be there by two."

She hung up and shut down her laptop then went upstairs to find something special to wear to the Nilsen's place.

At two o'clock, Carly pulled into the driveway of the Nilsen family lake home. She pulled out her phone. When Annika answered, she said simply, "I'm here."

The window of Annika's bedroom on the second floor slid up. "Hey, it's about time! I'm going crazy up here by myself," she called down. "Come on up. Get a couple of bottles of water from the fridge on your way! The doctor says I need to stay hydrated."

Carly went in the back door, grabbed the water bottles out of the stainless-steel side-by-side refrigerator, and took the stairs to Annika's bedroom. Annika lay on a pink patchwork quilt on her queen-sized bed watching a large television mounted on the wall. She picked up the remote and turned it off when Carly appeared in the doorway.

"Well, look at you," Annika said, as she tossed the remote aside and sat up wearing a long yellow nightgown. Her ice blonde hair had been braided into a thick rope that hung to her waist. She gave Carly a thorough inspection. "High-heeled boots, skinny jeans, and a long, slinky sweater. Wow—you look terrific. If I didn't know better, I'd think you were trying to impress my brother."

They laughed and opened their water bottles.

"You know I always dress up and wear makeup when I go out," Carly argued good-naturedly. She'd taken extra care to style her long, dark hair and put on makeup today as well. "I never know when I might see a 'help wanted' sign around town and I want to look my best in case I get an interview on the spot."

Annika sat on the edge of her bed fiddling with her hair as though she had something pressing on her mind. "About getting a job... How would you feel about being my caregiver?"

"What?" Carly stared at her in surprise. "You mean like, work for you?"

Annika nodded. "Depending on how things go, I might need someone to help around the house until the baby comes and for a while afterward. It's the only way I'm going to convince my mother to let me go home. Alex is freaking out at the prospect of having to move in here until the baby is born. I'm sure he'll agree to hire you in a heartbeat. So, say yes."

"Sure," Carly replied with a shrug. "I could really use the money but honestly, I'd do it for free. You know I don't mind helping you out."

"No way are you going to do this for free," Annika said. She took a swig of frosty cold water. "You need a job and I need to hire some help. I don't want anyone else but you, so it's settled. I'll talk to Alex about it tonight."

They were watching a romantic comedy movie when Helen arrived home.

"I bought some lefsa from the bakery," she hollered up the stairs. "I'll warm up a couple of slices for you girls. Send Carly down here to fetch it."

Carly slowly went downstairs, feeling like she was walking on eggshells around Helen.

"Hello, dear," Helen said with a warm smile. She placed a plate containing two rolls of lefsa in the microwave and programmed the timer. "You look very nice today. Is that a new outfit?"

Helen's sudden sweet disposition made Carly wary. Helen had never been this nice to her. "Well...um...yeah, sort of..."

"The boys and Knut will be home soon," Helen said as she pulled a loaf of bread from a grocery bag. "How would you like to stay for dinner tonight? We're having a fish fry. There's always room for one more."

"Um...well, I—"

The microwave dinged.

"Great! I'll put an extra setting on the table." Helen opened the door and pulled out the plate. "By the way, Erik and I had an interesting talk the other day...about Rylee...and you," she said in a low, motherly voice. "He said you were concerned that he'd told me the truth about her adoption, but you needn't worry." She moved close. "Your secret is safe with me."

Carly winced, wondering if it really was.

# Chapter Nine

Erik walked into the kitchen with Alex at four o'clock and was stunned to find Carly standing at the kitchen sink peeling potatoes.

"You and Alex—get those Walleye cleaned," Helen barked at him. "Tell Dad to set up the equipment. I'll dip the filets in cornmeal coating so he can deep fry them in the cooker outdoors. I want them crispy, hot, and on the table by five-thirty on the dot!"

"Yes, ma'am," he said wryly. "I'll be sure to relay your orders to Dad."

Carly paused from peeling potatoes as she turned her head and grinned at him. He grinned back. He didn't need to ask. He guessed she was staying for dinner.

He went outside, breathing a sigh of relief. His heartfelt talk with Helen had convinced her to keep his situation with Carly and Rylee private. To his surprise, she'd even softened her stance with Carly. He couldn't wait to spend a few minutes alone with Carly after dinner. He had something special he wanted to share with her.

As Helen had instructed, at five-thirty the family sat down at their dinner table piled high with food. Erik made sure he sat next to Carly. During the meal, they didn't say much to each other, but it didn't matter. Being with her, and sharing simple, everyday activities with her felt so natural, he wanted more of this. Always.

After dinner, Annika went back upstairs to lie down until dessert was served, and Erik helped Carly load the dishes into the dishwasher.

"I'll bet you never had to load your own dishes when you lived in L.A.," Carly said with a laugh as she scrubbed out a large saucepan. "Or clean your own fish."

"Not there," Erik replied. "I had a housekeeper who cooked for me and a gardener, and Hollywood stars living on both sides of me, but compared to the life I have here, it was a lonely and isolated existence. I had to come full circle to realize I already had everything I could possibly want right here." He looked into her eyes. "Everything."

She stopped scrubbing and stared at him. The softness in her smile indicated she was coming around to his way of thinking. He couldn't wait to get her alone.

"Ahem." Helen stood behind them holding an empty coffee carafe in her hands. "Hurry up with those dishes. We're going to have warm apple pie and ice cream in the living room as soon as the coffee is done."

"We're almost finished here," Carly said as she filled the carafe with cold water and poured it into the coffeemaker's reservoir. Getting back to business, she added decaf coffee grounds and started the coffee brewing.

After they finished dessert, Helen and Knut went into the family room to watch television. Alex and Annika went upstairs to spend the rest of their evening in privacy. Erik and Carly sat together on the wide swing on the front porch wearing hoodies and holding hands while staring at the full, orange moon in the sky.

"It was a big surprise when Helen asked me to stay for dinner," Carly said sincerely. "And she was nice about it, too, but as soon as I thanked her for the invitation, she handed me a bag of potatoes and the peeler."

They laughed loudly.

"She may be retired from running a café, but my mother will always be the boss," Erik said honestly. "It's just who she is. But she's trying to adjust her attitude about the things she can't change. Like me. Once she learned to accept me for who I am and stopped calling my songs 'devil music,' our relationship began to heal." He slid his arm around her. "Now that she knows about Rylee and what you went through, she's changed her attitude toward you, too."

"What about you, Erik?" She looked up at him, her eyes filled with uncertainty. "What is your attitude toward me?"

"I love you, Carly," he said and pulled her close, inhaling the sweet scent of her hair. "I always have. I've carried your memory on my arm ever since we broke up. Even though we were miles apart, you were always with me. You were always on my mind."

"I think you need to get it removed," she whispered as his lips brushed hers. "Or at least have it redone with a new design that says 'Carly and Erik. Forever.'"

He tightened his arms around her. "Whatever you say, baby." He crushed his lips upon hers as his heart poured out his desire to make up for a decade of loneliness and regret.

She drew in a deep breath and pulled back. Filtered light through the sheer curtains in the living room cast a silvery shadow on her face, catching the tears glistening in her eyes. "I love you so much, Erik. I never stopped. That's why it hurt so badly when you left me without finding out that I was pregnant with Rylee and why I wouldn't have anything to do with you after you came back. I didn't believe that you still cared about me after years of no contact. I didn't want to get hurt again."

"I told you this once before and I still mean it," Erik said as he framed her face with his hands. "I promise I'll never leave you again. Making music is my profession and it always will be, but you and my daughter are my life. You and Rylee will *always* come first."

He held her close, gently rocking the porch swing in the calm, still November evening. Traffic on their road had ceased hours ago. The only sound they heard was the slight creaking of the swing moving back and forth and the slow, methodical lapping of the lake upon the shore.

Erik breathed in the crisp fall air and stared up at the moon, glowing like a huge pumpkin in the sky. He was glad the band had been forced to come back to West Loon Bay. This sleepy little town perched on the shore of a huge, deep lake was his home, and the way his life was meant to be. No screaming crowds, no living out of a suitcase, no paparazzi invading their lives or pressure to produce another hit. This was where they would compose their best work because this was their paradise. Now that he and Carly were back together, his life had come full circle.

Their future could only get better.

\*   \*   \*

November 17th

"I don't like this," Alex said as he and Erik walked toward the pool hall. "We shouldn't be meeting him in public. This is a private conversation."

"I told him that, but he insisted," Erik said and stood aside as he opened the door. "I think he figures he'll loosen us up with a couple of rounds of beers and a few games of pool. Get us in the mood to listen to his proposal."

Alex stopped in the doorway. "I'm not in the mood to listen to anything if it means leaving Annika."

Erik nodded and followed Alex into the pool hall. At the far end of the room, Jonas stood leaning over a billiard table with a pool stick in his hands, getting ready to take a shot. He wore a dark green T-shirt and jeans. His thick dark curls brushed the nape of his neck.

They slid into their favorite corner booth and waited for his game to finish. A few minutes later, Jonas joined them.

"You guys want a beer?" he asked as he signaled for the waitress to bring him another one.

Erik held up his glass of Coke for a refill. He wanted to be completely straight for this meeting. So did Alex. In a few minutes, either they would reaffirm their original agreement, or the band would move forward minus one member. Whatever happened, so be it. They weren't budging from the original agreement. Either of them.

The waitress dropped off their refills and left their table. Since it was Jonas who called the meeting, Erik and Alex waited for him to start.

"We've been in town for six months. Doing nothing to promote the band. We need to start planning our next tour," Jonas announced and took a swig of his beer.

"We will someday," Erik said, "but the band has agreed to take a year off."

"I understand that," Jonas argued, "but nothing is stopping you from starting to plan the tour now."

"Yes, there is," Alex said as he leaned forward, his dark eyes hardening. "My wife is having a baby. I'm not going to even *think* about making any plans until my kid is born."

"Have you talked to Gunnar and Gabe?" Erik asked in an effort to diffuse the tension.

Jonas nodded.

"What did they say?"

Jonas stared pointedly at Alex. "They said they'd go along with whatever the three of us decided."

Alex sat back, his white-knuckled hands gripping the table. "I vote no."

Alex and Jonas both stared at Erik.

"Look," Erik said, trying to keep the peace. "By the time the agreement is up, Alex and I will have enough songs ready to produce a new album. We'll get together at that time and set up a production schedule. Once we get that set, we can work on the tour." Erik shrugged. "I mean, what's the use in going on a tour now if you don't have new material? All you'll be doing is recycling the old stuff."

Jonas folded his arms, frowning. "Every day we spend in this dump of a town, out of sight, we lose popularity because our fans are finding new bands to follow and losing interest in us."

"Not true," Erik shot back with a wry laugh. "Our sales are holding steady."

"The media is saying that we've disappeared," Jonas countered. "Don't you see how bad that is for our image? It's as though they're suggesting we've simply given up at the pinnacle of our careers."

"We'll have our media people put together something for us to keep in touch with our fans. Like a series of short videos to post on holidays or something to show we're on a long R&R and cast a few hints about our future plans," Alex replied, sounding bored. "Are we done yet?"

Jonas glared at him. "Yeah," he said and spat a few cuss words. "We're done here." He smacked his hand on the table and stood up. "If I find a better offer, we're done for good."

Last was the last straw. Erik stood up, getting in Jonas' face. "Are you threatening us?"

Jonas didn't back down. As he faced off with Erik, his green eyes glittered with challenge. "I'm putting you all on notice, Nilsen. Got that? I'm tired of this town. I've got better things to do than waste my time hanging around with farm boys." He turned and stalked out.

Erik exchanged a silent look with Alex, agreeing with him to finish their conversation in the car. They walked through the pool hall ignoring the stares of onlookers and made their way to the front door, observing Jonas through the large windows stretching across the front of the room.

Jonas stepped out of the building and froze. Standing in the middle of the wide sidewalk, he stared down the street, his eyes wide with shock.

"You look like you've seen a ghost," Erik said carelessly as he passed by, though not really caring.

"He did," Alex remarked evenly as they walked to his car. "Didn't you catch her? Isabella Dahl. The blonde who just crossed the street and walked into the law office."

Erik glanced across Main Street at the glass door to the law office but didn't see anyone. "Isn't that the girl everyone used to call rag doll because her family was so poor?"

"I never did, but I heard that other people in this town took pleasure in the cruelty of it," Alex replied with a shrug. "Jonas had a crush on her in school. Wanted to take her to the junior prom. His parents shut it down."

"I wonder how she's doing now," Erik said curiously as he reached the passenger side of Alex's car and placed his hand on the door handle, waiting for Alex to unlock the car. "I heard she left town right after graduation. Got a scholarship from some expensive private college in the Twin Cities."

Alex pointed past the windshield at a red BMW convertible parked next to them. "See for yourself."

Erik whistled and bent down, peering through the window. "That thing is *nice*. I wonder if she'd let me take it for a spin."

Alex laughed. "In your dreams, buddy."

Erik carefully opened the car door to avoid putting a ding in Isabella Dahl's "cherry" Beamer. He stuck his long leg inside Alex's vehicle and gripped his hand on the top of the door to ease himself inside. On his way in, he glanced over the roof of the car toward the pool hall.

Jonas Strom stood in the same place as before, his hands jammed into his pockets as he stared at the law office with his mouth open. His eyes had a stunned, faraway look. Like he'd seen a ghost.

Isabella Dahl obviously didn't know it, but her fleeting presence had turned that bad boy into a blithering idiot.

# Chapter Ten

Carly stared at the clothes bulging out of her closet, wondering what to wear tonight. She had a lot of outfits for every occasion, but she couldn't make up her mind as to what look she wanted. Erik said he'd pick her up at five o'clock. They were going to Summerville for dinner and a movie—their first official outing in public. People would be snapping pictures of her and Erik to post on social media, so she wanted to look her very best.

When word got out that she and Erik were back together, the paparazzi would come back to West Loon Bay in a flood to get the scoop as they did with Alex's engagement to Annika. Now that Carly found herself in the crosshairs of the public eye, she realized why Alex wanted to keep the wedding small and hold it in a remote location like Enchanted Island.

Alex and Erik were personal friends with Shawn Wells, the owner of the Morganville Hotel from their days of touring and staying at the Wells Corporation hotels. By hiring a private plane, providing the limos, and reserving every room in the hotel for wedding guests only, Shawn managed to keep the wedding completely secret until Alex's PR people released the official pictures online the next day.

Yeah…no such luck with that tonight. Many of the people seated around them in the restaurant would be taking pictures with their phones and posting them on the "Your Town" social media app for West Loon Bay.

Her phone chirped. It was a text from Erik. Flopping across her bed, she opened her phone and touched the green text button.

*Looking forward to tonight, babe. See u at 5. Luv u!*

She texted back, *Can't wait. Luv u 2!*

Dropping the phone next to her on the bed, she sighed and pulled the blanket over her shoulders. She hadn't slept a wink all night, thinking about Erik and how much her life was going to change now that they were together again. Especially when she told her friends and family. Annika would be the first to know. She'd give her parents the news right before Erik showed up at the house so they wouldn't have a chance to object. The fact that they would object at all made her sad but she knew they weren't willing to let go of the past so easily. The stressful thought made her more tired than she already was.

*This bed is so comfy. I'll just take a ten-minute snooze,* she thought drowsily and pulled the blanket over her ear. *Then I'll get up and get going. Just a little while…*

Her phone rang, startling her. Groggy, she located the phone and pressed the speakerphone. The caller ID read ARL, short for Annika Rae Lange. The phone's digital clock indicated she'd been asleep for over an hour.

"Hi!" she mumbled sleepily. She moved her hand away from the phone and closed her eyes. "I'm glad you called. There's something I want to tell you."

"Oh, really?" Annika said with a steely note of anger in her reply. "Aren't you a little late? Like ten years late?"

"What do you mean," Carly said through her sleep-induced haze. "What are you talking about?"

"We promised to tell each other our deepest secrets—before we told anyone else," Annika snapped, her voice shaking with hurt and disappointment. "I told you about the baby even before I told Alex because that's what *best friends do*. How could you do this to me, Carly? How could you conceal from me the fact that you had a baby with my brother? Did you think I wouldn't care? Or didn't my feelings matter?"

Her mind became instantly, fully awake. *Oh, no...* She bolted upright throwing off the blanket. "Annika, please, it's not like that. I didn't deliberately withhold it—I'm so sorry. Nobody knew about it except for my parents. That's the way they wanted it. They don't even know that I finally told Erik. Then Helen somehow got it out of him. She wasn't supposed to—"

Annika gasped. "You mean, even she knew about it? You told my mom, but not me?"

"No!" Carly sprang from the bed and began to pace the floor. "Annika, I never told your mom. She found out by accident. Listen," she said, running her fingers through her messy bun. "I'm coming over right now and I'm going tell you the whole story. Every bleeping minute of it from day one until today. Nobody knows that level of detail. Not even Erik. You're my best friend and you have the right to know."

"Too little, too late," Annika replied acidly. "You're no friend of mine. Not anymore."

The line went dead.

Carly fell back on the bed, crying. "Oh, dear God! What am I going to do? Trying to keep Rylee's identity a secret is going from bad to worse," she sobbed. "I feel like such a traitor. Annika is my best friend. I should have told her the truth years ago."

Annika had sounded so hurt, so betrayed. Did Erik break down and tell her? Who else could it have been? But...that didn't sound like him. He would have had her by his side when he told everyone—at once. Then, who did? What a screwed-up way to start a relationship. What an absolute disaster!

"Everybody has always been so worried about Rylee's well-being, but what about mine?" She squeezed her eyes shut, uttering a silent sob. "Doesn't anybody realize how deeply gut-wrenching and heartbreaking this has been for me? Does anybody *really* care?"

Tears began to flow from the corners of her eyes into her hair. All of the stress and hurt were finally coming out, but it didn't feel good to get it out of her system. It felt like her world was breaking apart.

Her phone beeped. Desperately hoping to find a text from Annika having a change of heart, she grabbed the phone and stared at it.

She blinked.

A post from the town's social media app popped up with a picture of Erik, Alex, and Jonas sitting together in a corner booth at the pool hall. The looks on their faces indicated they were embroiled in a serious conversation. The headline read "Wolfmoon is planning a world tour!"

"*What?*" She sat up again, reading the post by one of the guys who'd supposedly heard them discussing it in the pool hall. According to the poster, the trio had specifically met at the pool hall to plan a world tour around a new album. Right after Alex's baby was born.

"That's only seven months from now. Next June..." she said aloud. She tapped the link and watched a short video clip of Erik talking to Jonas about it. "What happened to their sabbatical? What about Alex's new house and Erik's plans to buy some land?"

She found Erik in her contacts and rang his number.

"Hey," he said affectionately. "How are you doing? Do you want me to pick you up early?"

She closed her eyes. "We need to talk."

He paused at the ominous tone in her voice. "What's wrong?"

"Not on the phone," she said. "I'll meet you at Frohn's Peak in ten minutes."

She hung up, not giving him a chance to question her further. Grabbing her purse, her phone, and her keys, she headed downstairs to slip into her jacket and drive her car to meet with him privately, not caring how badly she looked. Her face and hair weren't half as wrecked as she was inside.

She raced all the way to Frohn's Peak. Late spring through early fall, the peak provided a fantastic view of the vast waters of Lake Tremolo and the dense forests that surrounded it. During the day, tourists and school groups visited for educational purposes. At night, the remoteness of the site made it a prime spot for kids to party and lovers to take advantage of the privacy. It was on that very spot that her dad caught her and Erik in the back of his van when she failed to make it home by her curfew.

Erik was already there waiting for her when she drove onto the gravel parking lot. Wearing gray cargo pants and a matching fleece jacket, he jumped out of his pickup as soon as he saw her. Once she stopped her car, he pulled open her door. "Carly, what's wrong?"

"A couple of things," she replied as she shut off her SUV and got out of the car. Overhead, the gray November clouds were darkening. "First, I want to know how your sister found out about Rylee."

He stared at her looking totally flummoxed. "I don't know. Didn't she say where she got the information? Why are you asking me?"

"It had to be someone close to her," Carly said. Zipping her coat, she leaned her back against her vehicle. "You're the *only* person who could have told her."

"It must have come from my mother—"

"Ah, no it didn't," Carly retorted as a large snowflake floated past them. "Annika was upset with me when she found out that Helen had been told and she hadn't." She drew in a deep, tense breath. "It came from you, didn't it?"

"No!" He shook his head. His face grew crimson with indignation. "I told you, I didn't!"

She took his sudden reaction as a sign of guilt. "Right. Just like you promised me you'd never leave again."

Another large flake drifted downward between them.

He had the nerve to look confused. "What are you talking about?"

She glared at him. "The world tour, Erik."

He raised his palms in a gesture of innocence as if he didn't know a thing about it. "What world tour?"

She rolled her eyes in disgust. "The one that's plastered all over social media right now. You know, the one you and Alex went to the pool hall to plan with Jonas? The one you forgot to mention to me?"

He leaned one hand against the vehicle as if to brace himself. He seemed awfully nervous for someone who hadn't done anything wrong. "There is no world tour, okay? We were just talking."

"That's not what it sounds like to me or to the guy who posted it." She held up her phone and touched the video. It began to play.

*"Look," Erik said. "By the time the agreement is up, Alex and I will have enough songs ready to produce a new album. We'll get together at that time and set up a production schedule. Once we get that set, we can work on the tour." Erik shrugged. "I mean, what's the use in going on a tour now if you don't have new material? All you'll be doing is recycling the old stuff."*

"Carly, it's not what it sounds like," he argued. "You're hearing a snippet of the conversation, not the whole meeting."

"You should have at least given me the courtesy of hearing it from you instead of the internet," she said as angry tears formed in her eyes. "Is this how our future is going to shake out? Am I always going to be

85

your second most important consideration?"

"You're overreacting, Carly," Erik said, raising his voice. "If we go on tour, it's way into the future. There is a lot that goes into the planning, and we are nowhere near ready to start on it."

"Gee, thanks," she replied curtly. "I'll keep that in mind the next time I tune in to the internet to see what the band is doing."

"Look," he said with finality, "we make career decisions based on what's best for the band and it has nothing to do with you. It's business, understand?"

"Sure," she said quietly. "I get it." She jerked open her vehicle door and slid in. "Getting back together was a bad idea, Erik. I should have known that your old life would always be pulling you back—and away from me." She turned the key and started the car. "You're used to being in charge and you don't like your authority challenged. That may be the winning strategy for the band but not in a relationship. There is no room in your world for me. Or for Rylee. Go home. Dinner is *off.*"

She slammed the car door and shifted into reverse. Snow had begun to fall in large, feathery flakes.

"Carly, that's not true!" he cried. "You've got this all wrong. Come back!"

She tore out of the parking area and left him standing there, watching after her and shaking his head.

"Well, it's a good thing I found out who he really was before things got serious," she said as she drove through a burst of flurries. "He lied to me about talking to his sister and then he lied to me about his future plans with the band. I can't stay with a guy I can't trust."

Even so, her heart felt like it had a ten-pound rock sitting on it. Good things always took a long time, but disaster could explode without a moment's notice. Speaking of disasters, she wondered how long it would take before the press found out about Rylee.

The moment she walked into the house she sensed something was wrong. The atmosphere had a tense, tentative quality about it.

Darla burst into the kitchen wearing stretch jeans and a blue, cowl-necked sweater. Her short, dark curly hair had been loosely curled. "I tried to call you, Carly. Several times. Why didn't you answer your phone?"

"Sorry, Mom. It started snowing while I was driving. I needed to concentrate on the road, so I shut it off."

*In other words, I wanted to cry in peace.*

Darla grabbed her purse and pulled out her keys. "I was just about to leave without you. Edith is in the hospital."

"She's...in the hospital?" Carly stared at her mother in shock. "What happened?"

"I don't know." Darla turned off the kitchen light and opened the back door. "We'll find out when we get there. Let's go.

# Chapter Eleven

Erik drove his pickup home in a daze. If anyone would have told him that his happiness with Carly would be so short-lived, he wouldn't have believed it. She was wrong—about all of it, but he needed to apologize for how brusque he'd gotten with her over the tour. He was used to dealing that way with people in the business, but he'd been clearly in the wrong to talk to Carly like that.

Who told Annika about Rylee? He didn't have a clue, but he planned to find out who did. As far as the tour was concerned, the band's PR people needed to address the rumors that were now going to spread like wildfire.

Helen was on the house phone when he walked into the kitchen. The comforting aroma of warm banana bread filled his nostrils. Sadly, it was the only thing he found comforting right now.

"Okay, thank you," she said in a high-pitched voice and hung up. In the kitchen, she still used an old "Trimline" style phone from the 1980s in avocado green, attached to the wall with a long, coiled cord that stretched across the room.

"What's the matter, Ma?" he said gravely as he approached her. "Is Annika all right?"

"It's Edith Larsen," Helen replied with a tremor in her usually strong voice. "She's had a stroke."

All his life, his mother had operated the cafe with nerves of steel. She had to be that way for her business to survive. Seeing her on the verge of tears—again—worried him. He wasn't used to seeing her looking so frightened, so vulnerable.

"I'm sorry, Ma," he said and placed his arms around her giving her a heartfelt hug. "I know she's a close friend. Is there anything I can do to help?"

She pulled away. "Take me to the hospital. I need to find out how she is doing. No one in the emergency room will tell me over the phone."

"Okay," Erik said as he pulled out his keys. "Where's Dad?"

"He went to the Legion with Jim Torgerson to play in a cribbage tournament." Helen grabbed her purse and walked through the house to the foyer, stopping at the stairway to the second floor. "I'm going out for a while, Annika," she called up the stairs. "I'll be home later."

"Okay," Annika called back.

"There's no need to tell Annika about Edith until I get more information," Helen said as she entered the kitchen wearing her coat. She stopped. "She has enough to deal with right now. Is something wrong, Erik? You look sad."

"I'm good," he replied and opened the door for her. The last thing she needed right now was to hear about his problems. "We'll take my truck. The roads are getting slippery from the snow."

On the way to Summerville, Helen clutched her purse on her lap and stared out at the snow coming down so fast they could barely see the road.

"Edith called me this morning," she said suddenly. "She said she wasn't feeling well and she wanted me to come over. I assumed that she needed help with her housework, but she said there was something she wanted to tell me." Helen let out a deep, unhappy sigh. "I should have left right away, but I assumed she wanted to share some gossip so instead, I diddled around the house for a while, baking my banana bread and cleaning up the kitchen. By the time I arrived at her house, she was gone. Ida Sorenson came over and said Edith had just left in the ambulance."

Helen clutched a tissue to her face, wiping away tears.

"Don't beat yourself up, Ma," Erik said gently. "You had no way of knowing Edith was that sick."

"Yes, I did," Helen said quietly. "I've known for a while that she's been having issues with dizziness and headaches, and I've been helping her around the house on days when she's under the weather. I never mentioned it to her, but I wondered if it had to do with all the stress that she'd been going through recently with Carly violating the restraining order."

Erik shook his head. "That incident in the park was an accident. It's hard to avoid someone in a town as small as West Loon Bay, but since then Carly has intentionally kept her distance. Maybe Edith's health was declining for other reasons."

By the time they arrived at the hospital, a small group of people had gathered in the noisy, crowded emergency room to wait for word of Edith's condition. Several of her friends and neighbors huddled together drinking hospital coffee and discussing the situation among themselves. Pastor Bob, the senior clergy of Grace Lutheran Church in West Loon Bay stood with them. Ida Sorenson, Edith's elderly neighbor and close friend, had accompanied Rylee to the hospital. Rylee sat on a chair next to Ida wearing a bright red shirt with ruffles on the tops of the sleeves and silently watched everyone. Fear and uncertainty clouded her wide, blue eyes.

"How is Edith," Helen asked Pastor Bob as she rushed toward him.

The soft-spoken gray-haired man shoved his hands into his

pockets—a sign to Erik that the situation wasn't good. "We don't know," he said kindly. "We're still waiting for someone to give us an update on her condition."

Erik poured a cup of the hospital's complimentary coffee for Helen and one for himself. He took a sip of the hot liquid and grimaced. *Bleh…*

He walked over to Rylee and knelt on one knee to speak to her. "How are you doing, honey?"

She shrugged, seemingly too upset to speak as her eyes searched his. It broke his heart to see her so lost and unhappy.

He tugged at her long, braided ponytail. Wisps of reddish-brown hair framed her face and neck. "Are you hungry? Do you want something to eat?"

She shook her head.

He pulled a wad of one-dollar bills from his pocket and handed them to her. "Here. Take this—just in case you get hungry. Okay? There's a McDonald's across the street."

She slowly took the money. "Okay." Her words were so quiet he could barely hear her.

"What do you say," Ida said, prompting her. Tall and bony, the gray-haired woman wore a blue wool Nordic sweater with reindeer and rosemaling on it.

"Thank you," Rylee whispered.

"You're welcome, sweetheart." Erik stood and walked across the room to sit with his mother. Taking a seat, he pulled his phone from the pocket of his cargo pants and pulled up the news, bracing himself for a long day in this busy center.

His boredom didn't last long. Two minutes later, Carly and Darla Strand walked in. The moment Carly saw Rylee, she stopped, her eyes filling with panic.

Erik stood, desperate to talk to Carly, but Helen beat him to it.

"We're all waiting for news on Edith," Helen said to the women. "Would you like to sit down?"

Rather than answering, Darla Strand scanned the room but stopped when she saw Erik, her eyes growing cold, the skepticism on her face suggesting that he had no right to be there.

He stared right back, wanting her to know that he had every right to be there because *he knew* that Rylee was his and *he knew* what she and Dan and done to conceal it from his family.

Helen's expression turned stony when she saw their exchange, making it plain that she found Darla's attitude offensive. "Well," Helen added with a loud humph, "suit yourself." She sat down and folded her arms, stewing over the slight.

Carly took a seat as far away from Rylee as possible, respectfully keeping her distance, and avoided looking in Rylee's direction. It bothered Erik to see how worried Carly was about causing any issue with being around Rylee, but he doubted anyone in the room, other than her family, even knew about the restraining order. Most of the people in the emergency room were from Summerville and surrounding towns.

For a while, everyone settled down and waited in silence. Erik kept glancing at Carly, hoping to catch her eye, but she wouldn't look at him. He was engrossed in the daily paper when a small movement caused him to look up. Rylee stood in front of him wearing a hopeful look on her face.

"Will you take me to McDonald's?" she said quietly, wearing her coat.

"Uh... Did Ida say it was okay?" Erik cast a glance at Ida to confirm it.

Ida nodded. "I have trouble walking that far so I can't take her. Would you mind? It'll do her some good to get away from this depressing place for a while. Be sure to take her hand when you cross the street."

"Sure." Energized by the prospect of having dinner with his daughter, Erik tossed the paper aside and stood up. "Absolutely." He smiled down at Rylee. "Shall we go then?"

The little girl's smile warmed his heart.

Darla stood up looking uncomfortable with the arrangement. "You need some company?"

"Nope," Erik shot back cheerfully. "We're good." He wished Carly could come with them, but he would never do anything so reckless as to encourage her to violate a court order.

At the corner, he took Rylee's hand and walked her across the street. They went into the McDonald's and stood at the serving counter studying the menu overhead. He looked down at her. "What do you want?" He grinned. "A Big Mac with extra cheese?"

She held up a handful of dollars. "A happy meal."

"Okay." He waved her hand away. "I've got this. You keep that money for something else."

"I like Scholastic books," she said, warming up to him.

"That sounds like a good thing to spend it on."

Erik ordered the food and paid for the meal. They filled their drinks at the self-serv soda machine and found a booth by a window on the street.

Rylee diligently ate her meal but didn't have anything to say. At least she wasn't crying…

"Hey," he said, deciding to shake things up a little. "Can you do this?" He threw a French fry into the air and caught it in his mouth.

She grinned. "No."

"Aw, come on," he said with a chuckle. "You can do it! Watch again." He threw another potato strip into the air but this time it missed his mouth and bounced away.

Rylee laughed out loud. "See, you can't do it either!"

"Okay, I will this time." He tossed another French fry and caught it, chewing loudly. "See? You just have to practice."

Rylee picked up a French fry and tossed it, but it careened wildly and landed in the booth behind them. They both laughed and kept laughing as they acted out every parent's pet peeve—bad manners and playing with their food.

Slowly but surely, they were bonding. Of all the accomplishments Erik had achieved in his thirty years on this earth, this one was by far the most rewarding. And the one he valued the most.

By the time they finished eating, Rylee had slipped out of her low mood. Her face beamed with a wide smile. "Can we get dessert?"

Erik bought two ice cream cones and they set off walking back to the hospital.

"Do you think my mom is going to be okay?" Rylee asked and slipped her hand in his as they waited for the light to change.

"I don't know, sweetheart. I hope so," Erik said gently as he licked his cone.

They walked into the emergency room to find everyone in their party gone except Ida.

She stood up as soon as she saw them. "Did you have a good supper?" she asked Rylee.

Rylee nodded and kept licking her ice cream.

Erik stared at Ida, confused. "Where is everyone?"

Her smile faded. "Edith has been moved to intensive care.

Everyone went up there to keep abreast of her condition. I said I'd stay here and wait for you." She shook her head slightly to indicate Edith's prognosis wasn't good.

They took Rylee to the intensive care unit to see her mother. Most of the people in their group had already gone home, but Helen and Carly remained in the hallway. Erik smiled at Carly to let her know everything went well with Rylee.

Visibly upset, she turned and walked away.

Darla met them at the door to Edith's room. "Only one person at a time may visit her," she announced, sounding to Erik like the gatekeeper.

"When can I see my mom?" Rylee asked becoming impatient.

"I'll take you," Darla said and grabbed her by the hand.

"No," Rylee said in a whiney voice and pulled away. "I want Erik to come with me."

"Sure thing, kid," he said boldly with a smile. "Let's go."

*Get used to it, lady*, he thought as his gaze met Darla's. *I plan to be around for a long time.*

He shepherded Rylee into Edith's room to see her, but it wasn't the joyous reunion he had expected. Edith lay unconscious in her bed hooked up to too many tubes and beeping machines to count. He had no medical knowledge whatsoever, but anyone with common sense would conclude that Edith Larsen was barely hanging on to life.

What would happen to Rylee if she died?

*A court battle if it comes to that*, he thought grimly. *I don't know what the court will do in Carly's case, but if they deny her the right to her own child, I'll throw all the money I have after the best lawyers I can find to get custody. I'm not losing my daughter a second time.*

Clasping his hands together, Erik stepped back to allow Rylee some space. She moved to her mother's bedside and clutched the side as though afraid to touch the woman. She stood there silently for a while staring at her mother's pale, unresponsive face.

"Mommy," she said in a quiet voice. "Mommy, are you awake?"

Her words were met with silence.

"Mommy, can you hear me," Rylee asked and began to wail loudly. "Mommy! Wake up!"

Darla burst in. "She needs to leave." She grabbed the child by the hand. "Come on, Rylee, it's time to go."

"No!" Rylee screamed as she fought against Darla. "I want my *mom*!"

"Leave her alone," Erik said, pulling their hands apart. "This isn't the way to handle the situation."

"What would you know about it," Darla spat. "If you think you can show up after ten years and muscle your way into the situation, you're sadly mistaken. I don't care how rich you are. You don't have the right to interfere."

"We'll see about that." Erik turned away, surprised at the level of animosity Darla Strand held against him. It was unfortunate that she chose to be so bitter about the past, especially in front of Rylee, but that was her problem.

Ida met them at the door of Edith's room. "I think Rylee and I need to go home now," she said calmly. "We'll come back again tomorrow morning."

Erik followed them out. Once they were in the hallway, he turned to Rylee and held up his hand for a high-five. "Goodnight squirt. See ya around."

Through her tears, Rylee reached up and smacked his hand. "Bye," she said in a thick voice. "Thank you for the happy meal."

"My pleasure, sweetheart," he replied, fighting to keep his

emotions under control. It bothered him beyond words to see her so broken.

She waved at him as Ida led her to the elevator bank. He stood with his hands in his pockets, swallowing hard. He turned around and caught Carly staring at him. The message silently passing between them couldn't have been louder.

Their child's future happiness was all that mattered now.

# Chapter Twelve

Carly kept her distance and waited until the elevator doors closed on Ida and Rylee before she walked to the elevator bank and pressed the down button. After the scene she'd had with Erik earlier that day, she needed to keep her distance from him, too. She kept her gaze averted as they waited for the elevator to stop at their floor. Once it arrived, the foursome entered the car and silently rode it to the lobby. No one spoke until they passed through the automatic doors and walked down the sidewalk to the parking lot. Night had fallen and along with it, the temperature.

Carly and Darla charged ahead of Erik and Helen.

"I apologize if it's inappropriate to say this right now, but Carly, we need to talk about Rylee's future," Erik announced frankly.

Darla stopped at the curb and whirled around. "You've got a lot of nerve bringing this up before the poor woman has died. Where's your sense of decency?"

"That's rich coming from you," Helen cried. "The decent thing to do was to tell me that I had a grandchild, but you took it upon yourself to be judge and jury over that little girl's life! You kept her from knowing the other half of her family. Don't talk to us about decency!"

Carly turned back and slipped her arm through Darla's. "Mom, don't. He's right…"

"I'm sad about Edith," Erik said to Darla as he approached her. "She's a good woman and she doesn't deserve to go before her time, but she has a child who will be an orphan in a couple of days—possibly hours and we need to do everything we can to make sure that child ends up with at least one of her biological parents."

He looked at Carly. "We need to talk. Soon. As it is, Rylee is probably going to end up in a foster home until the court can sort it out. Do you agree that we need to act fast?"

Carly winced at the thought of Rylee being sent to live with strangers possibly in another town. Then she would never get to see her baby! "You know I do but I have no idea where to start. What do you suggest?"

"I'm no expert on the matter, either so I'm going to see an attorney as soon as possible and start the proceedings to establish paternity," Erik said in a humble, straightforward manner. "The test only takes a few days and if it's possible, I'll pay to have it expedited. Once that's done, I'll proceed from there."

Darla snarled at him. "Why don't you go back to whatever rock you crawled out from and leave us alone? Like I told you before, we don't need your interference."

"Me?" Erik snorted. "You've been interfering since day one. It's not your call any longer so I suggest you stay out of it."

Darla stepped forward, shouting in his face. "Somebody had to clean up your mess!"

"Mom," Carly said as she tugged on Darla's arm, "please, don't go there. Erik is right. Rylee's future is in his hands now. He has the money and the power to open doors that have always been closed to me. He's the one most likely to get custody of Rylee and we have to support his effort to give her a good life."

Erik's brows furrowed with alarm as he reached out to hold her hand. "Carly, I'm not trying to take her away from you. I want us to raise her together—"

"No," Carly said as she backed away. "You hold all of the cards. No court is going to grant me the right to visitation with my record of interference." Her shoulders slumped. "Even if I wanted to fight for her, I don't have a job or a penny to my name."

All she'd ever wanted was to be reunited with her child. All she'd ever dreamed of was to hear Rylee call her "Mommy." Sadly, it was all in her head. It was never meant to be.

"Your past doesn't matter," Erik argued. "I'll grant you the right to see her any time you want. You're her mother. She needs you now more than ever."

*And I need her!*

With tears in her eyes, she began walking toward the car. "Do whatever you need to do on Rylee's behalf, Erik. I won't cause you any trouble."

"Carly, wait," Erik begged as she walked away. "Don't shut me out. I want you to be a part of the process."

*Why*, she thought miserably, *so I can witness another person being granted the privilege to tuck my daughter into bed every night instead of me?*

She ran to the car and climbed in, slamming the door on the conversation.

Darla walked swiftly to the car and slid behind the wheel, jamming her key into the ignition. "Who do they think they are?" She started the car and tore out of the parking lot. "Where were they when the tough decisions needed to be made?"

"I don't know," Carly said solemnly, "but I think we made a

mistake by not telling Helen and Knut about it."

Darla laughed though her voice sounded far from mirthful. "Helen would have simply blamed you. Her son is and always will be perfect in her eyes!"

That was far from the truth, but Carly knew it was pointless to remind Darla how long it took Helen to accept Erik into her family again after he came back to town. She'd disapproved of his tattoos, his music, and his former life but eventually, she came around. Now, she was defending him like a mama bear.

In a lot of ways, Erik was just like Helen. As the saying went, the apple didn't fall far from the tree. He had her astute head for business and her strong work ethic. No wonder his band had made so much money over the years. A slice of that money, she noted, Rylee would someday inherit.

The knowledge that her daughter had a wealthy father and that she would soon become heir to his millions gave Carly a profound sense of relief. Regardless of the gossip that was bound to circulate about her birth, Erik would insulate her from it as much as he could. When Rylee became of age, she could attend an ivy league college and travel the world. Her father's money would give her independence. She wouldn't find herself stuck in the town from nowhere and schlepping beers for a living every weekend at a dive called The Ramblin' Rose. Like her mother.

And that was why she had no choice but to let Rylee go.

*   *   *

November 26th

The funeral for Edith Larsen was a huge affair on a cold, overcast day, the Saturday after Thanksgiving. Nearly the entire town turned out for her memorial service and the internment of her ashes. Darla and Dan Strand worked with Paster Bob to honor her memory with a wonderful service and a potluck reception afterward. However, because the town didn't have a reception hall large enough to hold all the people, they used the high school gymnasium and cafeteria with overflow in the hallways. Many attendees donated card tables and chairs to fill up the open spaces.

Carly spent the afternoon working in the cafeteria with her mother and her church's funeral committee to coordinate the huge influx of food and beverages donated by the attendees. They had so many crockpots lined up on tables lining the walls that a couple of the women on the committee had to send their husbands home to get power strips to get them all plugged into the electricity.

Ida Sorenson still had Rylee in her care, and they were seated at a table designated especially for the family. That meant Carly, too, but she purposely kept herself so busy she barely got a glimpse of them during the entire afternoon. She had no idea whether or not the restraining order was still in effect now that Edith was gone, but she wasn't taking any chances. Chief Wyatt was in attendance and the last thing she wanted to do was get herself arrested at her cousin's funeral!

Toward the end of the afternoon, after most people had left, Rose Lange stood at the beverage table pouring herself a cup of coffee. She wore a black western suit with a white oxford blouse and her signature turquoise jewelry. She waved to Carly through the cafeteria serving window.

"Hi, Rose," Carly said to her former employer and close friend as she left the kitchen and approached the table. "How are you doing?"

"Hello, Carly," Rose said kindly. "How are *you* doing? You okay?"

"I'm fine," Carly replied, though she knew she wasn't fooling Rose. That woman knew her like a book.

Rose leaned close. "Can you get away for a couple of minutes? I'd like to have a chat."

"Sure." Carly went back into the kitchen and told Darla she wanted to take a short break. She pulled off her apron, grabbed a fresh can of Coke, and followed Rose into the hallway to a table away from the lingering crowd.

The moment they sat down, the expression on Rose's face grew serious, indicating this was no social call. She had something on her mind. And when Rose had something on her mind, she didn't hold back.

Rose pushed her coffee aside and folded her arms on the table, jingling her turquoise and silver bracelets. "I heard that you and Erik Nilsen hit it off for a while and then you two had some sort of falling out."

Darn that Alex and his big mouth! He must have told her. According to Annika, he and his mother spoke nearly every morning on the phone while drinking their breakfast coffee.

"We had it out at Frohn's Peak."

Rose's golden brows shot up. "So, I heard."

Holy mackerel. What else had she heard?

"Do you love him?" Rose asked directly.

"All my adult life," Carly responded. No sense trying to make excuses. Rose was a tough woman who'd owned and managed The Ramblin' Rose Bar for twenty-five years. When she asked a direct question, she knew whether or not you were telling the truth.

"I can see it in your eyes," Rose said, her tone softening. "You've been hurt. Did he hit you? Is there another woman?"

Carly shook her head. "No, Erik would never do anything like that."

"Then go after him," Rose said sounding more like a mother than a friend. "Straighten things out between you."

"But Rose, he lied to me!"

Rose reached across the table and took her hand. "Honey, there are lies, and then there are *lies*. But the worst lies are the ones you tell yourself. Like the lie that retreating from the situation is for the greater good. Don't go there. Don't let this man go if he's the one for you." She squeezed Carly's fingers in encouragement. "What I'm saying is be strong. Fight for what you want. Don't make the mistake that I did."

Then she proceeded to tell Carly that years ago when she was a young woman, she broke off with a man because he was newly married, even though she was pregnant with Alex. She kept quiet about the identity of Alex's father for thirty years to protect the man's reputation and his family. Only to find out one day that he'd never stopped loving her and he'd been in an unhappy, difficult marriage all that time. Now, she and Hugh Wyatt were finally getting married and living the happily ever after they were always meant to have.

"If I tried to get back with him now," Carly said, "my background check might jeopardize his adoption of Rylee Larsen. I—I've had issues with someone and there is a restraining order on my record."

"She's your child," Rose said, sounding like a mother again. "And Erik's."

Carly nodded, admitting to Rose that her suspicions were true.

"Back in the day," Rose said, "you were convinced by well-meaning people that giving her up for adoption was the best option for the child, but it wasn't the best decision for you, was it?"

Carly almost swallowed her tongue. "You knew?"

"It wasn't hard to figure out. You and Erik used to come to the house to visit Alex in high school. It was obvious you two were in love. Rylee is the right age and frankly, she's a lot like you. When I heard he was adopting her, I simply put the facts together."

Clasping her hands together to keep them from shaking, Carly looked down at the table to avoid anyone seeing the sadness she knew showed on her face. "I've regretted it ever since."

"Think about it, Carly," Rose implored her. "Sometimes you only get one chance to make it right."

Her heart sunk at the thought. Her only chance had probably already passed her by.

# Chapter Thirteen

Erik couldn't get close to Carly at the funeral. With so many people there, he and his parents were way back in the crowd at the church. When everyone walked to the cemetery, they got pushed back even further.

With every day that passed, he missed her more. She was wrong about him on so many counts, but he couldn't talk to her about it—she'd blocked him on her phone. He'd considered parking outside the Strand home until she came out and talked to him, or going up to the door and pounding on it, demanding to speak to her, but with his court case pending to adopt Rylee, he didn't want to take the chance of having Darla or Dan call the police on him.

The DNA test had given him the results he needed to prove he was Rylee's father, and he began the legal process of adopting his biological child. He'd hired a private lab in Minneapolis for a quick turnaround and received the information in twenty-four hours. He kept in touch with Ida Sorenson, calling her every day to check on Rylee and visited her twice a week. Erik had convinced the county to allow the child to continue staying with Ida until the adoption became final. In the meantime, he worked with his lawyer to cooperate fully with the county and the court to move the process along.

Rylee's "orphan" status touched the hearts of many of the

townspeople in West Loon Bay. Volunteers cleared the snow from Ida's sidewalks and driveway, and neighbors dropped off casseroles and baked goods. The women's circle Bible study group from Ida's church took turns giving Ida transportation to church, the grocery store, and doctor appointments. Everyone who helped wanted to show kindness to Rylee and Ida in any way they could.

Erik was grateful to all who reached out to Ida, but it bothered him that the person who wanted to help the most, couldn't go near Rylee. Though it would take time for the adoption to go through, once he got custody of her, he planned to allow Carly to see her daughter any time she wanted. Rylee would get to be with her mom and he would get to see the woman he loved. Somehow, he would find a way to get through to Carly how much he still loved her for Rylee's sake—and for his.

\* \* \*

December 10th

Erik drove uptown to meet Alex for lunch at the pool hall. Alex and Annika were no longer staying at the house. Annika's condition had improved enough to allow her to move back into her own home provided she hire domestic help to take care of her and Alex. Having so many adults underfoot at their parents' home had been hectic and at times, stressful, but there were good times, too, like Sunday dinners, family movie nights, Thanksgiving dinner, and the night they decorated the Christmas tree. Even so, he was glad his sister was well enough to move back into her own home. At times, she could be quite a diva!

He pulled his pickup into a parking space on Main Street in front of the law office and met Alex at the pool hall. Alex sat in their favorite corner booth, waiting for him. The usual noisy contemporary rock and country tunes had been replaced with Christmas songs.

"Hi," Erik said to Alex as he slid into the wooden booth and dropped his keys on the table. "What's the special today? I'm starving."

Before Alex could answer, a slim brunette wearing jeans, a dark

T-shirt, and a short, black apron approached their table. She set a thick paper coaster in front of Erik. "Hi, Erik! What would you like to drink today?"

"Nothing for him, Kristin." Alex waved her away. "He's not staying."

"Alex, what are you doing?" Erik said and tried to get Kristin's attention again as she walked away from their table.

"Listen," Alex said in a low voice, leaning forward so the guys sitting in the next booth couldn't hear him. "I've got a hot tip for you. Carly has an appointment with Edith's attorney, and she's across the street sitting in his office right now. So, if you want to talk to her, this is the perfect opportunity."

Erik's pulse sped up at the prospect of talking with her one-on-one. "How do you know she's got an appointment?"

"Well, for one thing, I saw her walk in the door just before you drove up but I already knew she was going to be there."

"How would you know that?" Erik replied drily. "Are you tapping her phone or something?"

"I stopped by my mom's place this morning to pick up a maternity outfit she bought for Annika. She was on the phone with Carly talking about the appointment and encouraging her to go. She hung up right away when she saw me and didn't tell me who she'd been talking to, but I'd heard enough to know what was going on."

Erik glanced through the glassed-in front of the pool hall lined with Christmas lights at the law office across the street. Alex was right. It was make-or-break time. He grabbed his keys and slid out of the booth. "Thanks. I owe you one, buddy."

Alex sat back and picked up his menu. "My neck's on the line here for giving you confidential information. You'd better not mess this up!"

Erik left the pool hall and headed back to his pickup to wait for Carly to come out of the law office. Main Street looked like a scene in a Hallmark movie with evergreen boughs and velvet bows hanging on every streetlight. All of the shops, including the pool hall, were decorated with lights, small, potted Christmas trees, and huge snowflakes sprayed on the windows. As soon as he reached his truck, Carly appeared on the other side of the glass entry door. She stood in the entryway, reading something. He walked to the door and reached out to open it, but it suddenly swung open from the inside, forcing him to quickly step backward. Carly rushed out crying so hard she couldn't see where she was going.

"Hey, hey," he said with great concern as he stopped her and placed his hands on her upper arms to hold her still. "What's wrong?"

She looked up, her eyes swimming with tears. "Erik, what are you doing here?"

"I came uptown to have lunch with Alex and saw you... What's happened?"

She burst out in loud sobs. "I feel so guilty…"

"Listen to me, if this is about the adoption—"

She hung her head and continued to cry.

"C'mon," he said and pulled her toward his vehicle. The fact that she didn't object proved how distraught her appointment had left her. "People are staring at us. We're going to sit in my truck until you've settled down."

He opened the door and helped her in, ignoring the stares of curious onlookers. He wanted to take her someplace where they could be alone, but he didn't know if she would consent to leave with him so this would have to do. This might be his only chance to talk some sense into her. If it didn't work, he knew it was truly over between them. He had to let his feelings go.

He slid into the driver's seat, shut the door, and turned on the radio leaving the volume down. A little soft music in the background while he spoke to her was in order to infuse calm into an emotional situation. Elvis' melancholy voice sang the words "I'll have a blue Christmas without you..."

"Okay," he said softly and opened the center console, grabbing a couple of napkins for her to use as tissues. "What happened? Start from the beginning." He shut the console and leaned on it, using it for an armrest.

She held out a folded sheet of letterhead, offering it to him to read. He took it but didn't open it. He wanted to hear her story first.

"I got a call from Edith's attorney," she said as she scrunched the napkins into a ball and wiped her eyes. "He said he had a letter that she had written to me and he wanted to give it to me." She nodded to the wrinkled paper in his hand. "I figured it was her last chance to vent over the way I'd treated her, so I put off going to his office until today. I didn't want to read it in front of him so I went through it when I got downstairs instead. Like I said, I didn't expect much. I thought Edith wanted to get in the last word about leaving Rylee alone after she died, but that wasn't her intention at all..." Her face, already red and puffy, burst into a fresh round of tears.

Wondering what in the heck Edith said that had made Carly so upset, he opened the letter and began to read it.

*Dear Carly,*

*If you are reading this letter, then I have passed away.*

*I hope you have forgiven me for taking steps to keep you from disrupting our lives. I never meant to hurt you by keeping you and Rylee apart, but your interference caused me to fear that she might somehow learn the truth about her birth before she was old enough to understand. I am the only mother she's ever known, and I felt in my heart that it was wrong to turn her life upside down at such a young age.*

*I never doubted your love for her. I always knew Rylee would be better off with you because I was not in the best of health, but I was lonely—especially after Frank's death. She filled a large gap in my heart that his passing created. I pray that my death doesn't cause her the level of grief that losing Frank caused me, but if it does, loving her with all your heart will help it to pass. She is young. She will adapt.*

*Take care of our baby. Don't ever break her heart. Even though I didn't give birth to her, I've always cherished her more than my own life. My only goal was to see her grow up happy and healthy. It breaks my heart to think that I won't be there for her.*

*Please, don't ever give up on her. She needs you.*

*Your dearest cousin, Edith*

Stunned, he read it a second time. When he finished, he folded it carefully and handed it back to her. "She didn't want you to feel guilty," he said honestly. "She wanted you to understand that everything she did was in Rylee's best interest, but she didn't harbor any hard feelings over the issues between you."

"I shouldn't have caused her so many problems," Carly said as she shoved the letter into her purse. "If I'd stayed away, she might still be alive."

"Edith died from complications with her diabetes, Carly." Reaching into the backseat, he grabbed two bottles of water from an open package on the floor and handed one to her. "She'd been having problems for a while with dizziness and headaches. My mother used to help her around the house with cleaning and doing the wash on days when she didn't feel good. You didn't know about that?"

She shook her head, her eyes wide with surprise. "I knew what she'd died from, but I didn't know that she'd had ongoing problems beforehand."

"The day she died, she called in the morning and asked Helen to come over. Edith had something important she wanted to tell her," he said as he twisted the cap off his water bottle.

Carly shifted in her seat, facing him. "What was it?"

"Nobody knows," he replied and took a drink. "My mother figured it was some juicy gossip going around town so she took her time getting over there. When she arrived, Ida told her that the ambulance had just left."

Carly stared at her water bottle as though pondering Edith's last intended words. "Does Helen have any idea what it might have been?"

"No," he said, "but my guess is that Edith knew her time was getting short, and she wanted to get something off her chest." He started the truck and turned on the heat. "I think she was going to reveal to my mother that Rylee was her grandchild." He let out a wry chuckle. "If Ma hadn't already known, *that* would have caused an instant nightmare. Aren't you glad I spilled the beans instead of Edith?"

"Oh, boy," Carly said. "I guess I am. Helen would have been all over my parents about it and caused a huge stink. She would have had the whole town taking sides."

"She's not as bad as that," he said, dropping his voice low. "Things aren't always as they seem, Carly."

She gave him a guarded look. "What do you mean by that?"

"I didn't tell Annika about Rylee. She overheard us talking about it the night we were together on the porch swing. So, you see, I'm not your enemy."

She frowned as though his statement had hit a nerve. "I never said you were."

"No, but you *act* like I am."

"That's not true," she argued. "I don't hate you, Erik. I'm happy that you're going to adopt Rylee. H-how's that going?" She smiled to show him she was sincere, but at the same time, her hands shook so badly that she nearly dropped her water bottle as she twisted off the cap.

"It's moving along but it takes time," he replied. "I'm going to rent Edith's house from her estate until my new house gets built next year. That way when the adoption goes through, Rylee can move back into her original home with me. Ida will continue to help with watching her after school if I'm not able to make it home in time."

"Does Rylee know that you're her biological father?"

"Not yet," Erik replied. His chest tightened at the prospect of having to explain such a sensitive subject to his little girl. "For now, I call myself her 'new' dad and she likes that." He set his bottle in the cup holder and leaned toward her. "She asks about you every time I see her. She wants to know if you're coming to live with us, too. I promised her I'd ask you about it."

"Live with you?" She looked flustered, her deep frown indicating she didn't understand. "You mean, as her nanny?"

"No, I mean, as my wife," he said with tenderness. "Rylee needs her mom. I need *you*." Reaching over, he lovingly traced his finger slowly along her jaw and down the side of her neck. "I want my family together. This is what was meant to be. You, me and Rylee. I lost you both for ten years. I don't want to spend another minute without either of you." He kissed her slowly. "I'm asking you to marry me, Carly."

She blinked slowly. "What did you say...?"

He smiled as he slipped a soft wisp of errant hair behind her ear. "Something I should have said a long time ago and I'll keep saying it as long as it takes to convince you that I'm sincere. *Will you marry me, Carly?*"

It was getting hot in the pickup, or was it his blood pressure rising from desperation? He reached over and turned the key, shutting down everything but the soft, romantic voices of Andy Williams singing, "It's the most wonderful time of the year…"

"I've tried to move on, but I can't," he whispered. "I haven't stopped thinking about you since that day we split up at Frohn's Peak. I'm sorry for anything I said or did to make you mistrust me. When it comes to the band, I tend to get aggressive. Sometimes I get it wrong, but I'll always come back and try to make things right." With utmost gentleness, he slowly lifted her chin with his finger looking deeply into her beautiful brown eyes. "I still love you, Carly. More than ever. I want to be with you always. Marry me."

Her face flushed as though she found his proposal shocking, but she didn't shrink back or push his hand away.

Taking her hands in his, he pulled her close. "I want to spend the rest of my life with you. Build a big house in the country. Have a couple more kids." Brushing his lips across hers, he whispered, "I love you so much."

"You, me, and Rylee," she whispered as though she needed a moment to absorb what he was offering.

"To have and to hold, Carly," he said, reciting what he remembered the minister saying at Annika's wedding. "From this day forward—"

"*Yes.*" Desperation in her tearful brown eyes reflected like a mirror into her soul. Rising up on her knees, she leaned across the console and slid her arms around his neck to kiss him. "I love you too, Erik," she whispered, melting into his embrace. "I've been trying to get over you ever since I was seventeen, but I've failed at every turn. I can't get you out of my heart."

"Let's go away and get married. Somewhere exotic and romantic like Hawaii," he murmured in between kisses. "Just the two of us. No problems, no interference, just days of strolling along the beach and nights…*together*."

"I've always dreamed of seeing that place," she said breathlessly. "Going there with you would be amazing. When?"

"How soon can you get a bag packed?"

She pulled back, responding to his question with an incredulous laugh. "Today? Now? Are you crazy?" She pulled down the visor and checked her crimson, tear-stained face in the mirror. Her eyes were heavily smudged underneath from her mascara. "Ugh. I look like I've been run over by a truck. I can't go anywhere looking like this."

He slipped his fingers through her long silky hair. "You're beautiful just the way you are."

"What about the adoption? Erik, will marrying me create a problem with the court?"

"I don't know," he said as he kissed her, tightening his embrace. "We'll cross that bridge when we come to it and let our lawyer deal with the issue. For now, I just want to think about the two of us getting away from here. *Alone*."

"But…our parents. Erik, what are we going to tell them?"

He waved the idea away. "Who cares? We'll send them a postcard."

They burst out laughing. They had a lot of living—and loving—to do to make up for the time they'd lost, and Erik was determined to make every minute count. He loved her so much.

Their 'happily ever after' had already begun.

# Epilogue

Carly shut the door to her room and pressed a contact on her cell phone. She should have made this call weeks ago, but…better late than never. At least now she had something juicy to say to make up for committing the indefensible sin of holding back about Rylee.

"Yeah," Annika said sounding disinterested and annoyed.

*She saw my name on the caller ID, but she still answered the phone,* Carly thought as her heart fluttered. *I'll take that as a sign that she's willing to forgive me.*

"Are you ready for the secret of the century?" Carly boasted in a tantalizing tone as she pulled a large vinyl carry-on bag from her closet and dumped it on her bed.

Her question was met with a tentative silence.

She jerked open her underwear drawer and grabbed a few items, tossing them into the bottom of the bag. "I mean, hey, isn't that what best friends do? Tell each other amazing things?"

"What are you talking about," Annika asked curiously. "What amazing things?"

"Promise you won't tell *anybody*? Not even Alex until I say so."

"That depends," Annika said quickly, still annoyed. "This had

116

better be good."

Carly smiled to herself with hysterical happiness at the words she was about to say. "Erik and I are eloping."

No answer. Just a long, loud gasp.

"Today, in case you're wondering when it's going to happen. He's picking me up at the end of the block in…" she checked her sports watch. "Twenty minutes. Wow, I've got to hurry! Anyway, we're driving straight to the Twin Cities and taking a red-eye flight to Honolulu. He texted me a couple of minutes ago and said he bought the tickets. You are the *only one* who knows."

Annika chuckled. "Running away just like two teenagers. Do you want me to break the news to everyone for you?"

"That would be great! But not until I call you. Okay? I'll let you know when we're ready to board the plane."

A loud squeal pierced her ear. "What are you going to wear?" Annika asked with excitement.

"No idea," Carly said as she reached into her closet and pulled a couple of tops off their hangers. "I think I'm probably going to buy the dress when I get there. Maybe one of those strapless jobs with exotic flowers on it or something."

"And shoes!" Annika exclaimed. "Buy some gorgeous shoes!"

Carly grabbed her brush and dropped it into the bag. A small bottle of perfume got stuffed into her cosmetics bag. "Okay. I don't have room for them in my carry-on anyway."

"You'd better take pictures and text them to me *immediately*. Oh! And put a large white flower behind one ear before you take the picture, okay?"

"I promise," Carly replied. "You'll get the shots before the ink on our marriage certificate is dry."

"Oh, Carly, I'm so happy for you," Annika said tearfully. "You've been in love with my brother for a long time. It's about time you two found each other again. You, Erik, and Rylee are going to make a perfect family."

"Thanks, Annika. That means so much coming from you. Oh, my gosh. We don't have rings! We've got some serious shopping to do on the island!" Carly shoved a pair of shorts into her bag and her swimsuit.

"Hawaii sounds so romantic," Annika said with a wistful sigh. "I wish you and Erik all the best. Love you."

"Love you, too, Annika. Bye!"

For the next fifteen minutes, Carly hurried, picking up important items to stuff into her already full bag. She managed to zip it shut and sling it over her shoulder. Then she tiptoed downstairs to grab her coat and sneak out the front door while Dan and Darla were busy in the kitchen making lunch and watching the noon news.

She slipped out of the house and jogged down the block lugging her heavy bag. As promised, Erik's pickup sat parked at the end of the street. He jumped out when he saw her and grabbed her bag to stuff into the backseat.

Once they were both safely in the truck, he turned to her with a boyish grin. "Are you ready?"

"Yep, and *this time* my dad isn't going to catch us!"

They sealed it with a kiss then laughed as he stepped on the gas, taking them to the airport and a lifetime of adventures together.

### *The End*

But wait…there's more!

(Read on for exciting news of more books in this series!)

I hope you enjoyed **Brown-Eyed Girl,** the journey of Erik Nilsen and Carly Strand as they struggled to make sense of the issues they faced. This is book two of the West Loon Bay series and at this time, I have plans to write eight books in all. (Maybe more; we'll see!)

The next book, **Country Girl,** featuring Jonas Strom and Isabella Dahl will be out sometime in 2023. Ideas for a gripping plot are already forming and twisting in my head!

You can find the complete list and the covers for all of the books in the series on my website at htttps://www.deniseannettedevine.com

**Want to find more authors who write sweet romance?**

Join my reader group at Happily Ever After Stories – Sweet Romance. If you like sweet romance and want to be part of a great group that has lots of fun and fantastic parties, visit us at:

https://www.facebook.com/groups/HEAstories/

# More Books by Denise Devine

### Christmas Stories
Merry Christmas, Darling
A Christmas to Remember
A Merry Little Christmas
Once Upon a Christmas
A Very Merry Christmas - Hawaiian Holiday Series
~*~

### Bride Books
The Encore Bride
Lisa – Beach Brides Series
Ava – Perfect Match Series
~*~

### Moonshine Madness Series – Historical Suspense/Romance
The Bootlegger's Wife – Book 1
Guarding the Bootlegger's Widow – Book 2
The Bootlegger's Legacy – Book 3
~*~

### West Loon Bay Series – Small Town Romance
Small Town Girl – Book 1
Brown-Eyed Girl – Book 2
Country Girl – Book 3 (Coming in 2023)
~*~

### Cozy Mystery
Unfinished Business
Dark Fortune
Shot in the Dark (Girl Friday Series)
~*~

This Time Forever - an inspirational romance
Romance and Mystery Under the Northern Lights – short stories

*Want more? Read the first chapter of each of my most popular novels on my blog at:*
**https://deniseannette.blogspot.com**

Made in USA - Kendallville, IN
27140_9781943124374
10.04.2022 1406